Crystal
Hawke

"You Got a Letter!"

Rita burst into the Dawson kitchen. She handed the envelope to Elizabeth.

Nine days had passed since Elizabeth mailed the five applications and five photographs. Her heart pounded. This was it.

"Open it!" Rita demanded.

Elizabeth stared at the white rectangle. It was regular letter size. Was that a good sign?

"Don't rush me, Rita. This could be the most important letter of my life. It could be the beginning of my professional career—or the end of it."

Elizabeth sat down at the table. She held the envelope. It was light. She took a deep breath, then opened it slowly. Pulling the sheet out, she took a few more deep breaths. Carefully, she unfolded the paper and began to read.

Elizabeth's eyes widened. "I don't believe it!"

D0048183

Most Archway Paperbacks are available at special quantity discounts for bulk purchases for sales promotions, premiums or fund raising. Special books or book excerpts can also be created to fit specific needs.

For details write the office of the Vice President of Special Markets, Pocket Books, 1230 Avenue of the Americas, New York, New York 10020.

Judith Eichler Weber

LIGHTS, CAMERA, CATS!

**illustrated by
PAT GRANT PORTER**

AN ARCHWAY PAPERBACK
Published by POCKET BOOKS • NEW YORK

For my children, in order of appearance:
Daniel, Jeffrey, and Fifi, the cat

 An Archway Paperback published by
POCKET BOOKS, a division of Simon & Schuster, Inc.
1230 Avenue of the Americas, New York, N.Y. 10020

Text copyright © 1978 by Judith Eichler Weber
Illustrations copyright © 1978 by Pat Grant Porter

Published by arrangement with Lothrop, Lee & Shepard Company
Library of Congress Catalog Card Number: 78-17083

All rights reserved, including the right to reproduce
this book or portions thereof in any form whatsoever.
For information address Lothrop, Lee & Shepard Company,
105 Madison Avenue, New York, N.Y. 10016

ISBN: 0-671-46858-8

First Archway Paperback printing February, 1984

10 9 8 7 6 5 4 3 2 1

AN ARCHWAY PAPERBACK and colophon are
trademarks of Simon & Schuster, Inc.

Printed in the U.S.A.

IL 4+

1

THE ALARM RANG. ELIZABETH TRIED to stretch her legs but the lumps at the bottom of her bed refused to move. She gave a sharp kick. Alexander the Great, a large red-haired tomcat, jumped off and walked arrogantly out of the room with tail held high. Cat, the oldest member of the bed mates, ignored Elizabeth's flying feet. Princess Margaret yawned and stretched. Then she started to lick her long white hair. The other two smaller cats, Tinker Bell and Butch, took the leg movements as a signal to play.

Elizabeth pushed down the button on the alarm clock and jumped out of the bed.

"Out you go!" she said and shook the bed until it was empty of cats. Then she held onto the headboard and did a few high kicks.

"Breakfast in ten minutes," her mother called from the downstairs hall.

Elizabeth pulled back the light-blue organdy curtains and opened the blinds. Then she pushed the window up just enough to be able to put her head out. She shivered. It was a clear but chilly April day. Branches from the oak tree almost touched her second-story window. She looked over the garage and into the Shaws' backyard. She stretched to see her best friend's house. Rita's shade was still down. Yep, she thought, I beat her again. She left the blinds open to signal her victory. Then she closed the window and started to dress.

In a few minutes Elizabeth was running through the house. She stopped at the front hall and picked up the television section of the newspaper. Her father always left it for her before he went off to make the 8:05 Edge Valley commuters' special to New York City. He was the New Products Director at the Purrfect Cat Food Company. She wished he could drive her to school as some of the fathers did, who didn't work in the city.

"Only one week and three days and I'll almost be a teen-ager," she said to her mother.

"Elizabeth, you're making such a fuss about turning twelve." She tied a stained apron over her powder-blue sweater and matching slacks. Her hair was held back by a chiffon scarf. Elizabeth thought her mother looked great, but she didn't tell her so.

"Well, it's sort of speical. It's the very, very

tail end of childhood and the beginning of being grown up." Elizabeth sat down and poured cereal into her bowl. For a moment she watched her mother's graceful figure with envy. "Mom, I want to talk to you about my gift."

"Fine, dear, but talk quickly or you'll miss the school bus. I can't leave the house to drive you today because I'm expecting a large order of antiques."

"Do you think Daddy would be crushed if I didn't get another kitten this year?" She was tired of receiving a kitten every birthday. Five kitty litters to clean was enough!

"Elizabeth, you know it's a tradition."

"But I have ten cats! If you don't count George, who's been missing for months."

"George really isn't missing, dear. He just couldn't stand all the competition around here and probably found a quieter home. George was, I mean is, too smart to be missing."

"Mom, that's not the point and you're changing the subject. Could I skip the kitten this year? The skateboard is enough."

"But cats are so important to your father's business," Mrs. Dawson said with a sigh. Elizabeth knew that he liked to try new product ideas on them. But she was the one stuck with taking care of them.

"Remember when he thought soup for cats would be great and none of ours would eat it," Elizabeth said, and chuckled.

"But the collars that glow in the dark were a successful premium. And Dad thought of that idea the night we searched for Snow Flake."

"But my bed is getting crowded and I'm never alone."

"Elizabeth, you're always complaining about being an only child. Now you say you're never alone. Hurry up or you'll be late," Mrs. Dawson said.

"Will you talk to Daddy?" Elizabeth begged. She grabbed her lunch bag and stuffed the television section of the paper into her books.

"When you come home," her mother said, as Elizabeth put on her polo jacket, "I'll probably be in the basement sorting and polishing the antiques."

Mrs. Dawson had turned her hobby of collecting antique silver into a home business. Elizabeth was glad. Now her mother was less involved in the Parents' Association and wasn't hanging around school so much.

"Mom, am I ever going to get my ping-pong table back?"

"If I get a store. But for now, it's the perfect display table. You hardly ever used it anyway."

As soon as Elizabeth opened the front door she saw her friend Rita waving to her from the sidewalk.

"Hurry," Rita called. "We'll be late and I don't want to get in trouble again because of *you*."

"If you want to live a plain, ordinary, dull life don't be my friend," Elizabeth said.

"Giving flowers to our teacher was okay, but picking the tulips in front of the school library wasn't so smart, Elizabeth Dawson."

The big yellow school bus stopped at the corner. The girls ran to it and quickly boarded behind two younger boys.

"First of all," Elizabeth said, "nobody told me that tulips don't grow back until next year and second, it's the idea that counts!" Elizabeth found a window seat in the rear of the bus. She pulled out the television section of the paper, and ignored Rita who took a seat directly across from her. There on the inside page was a picture of Clarence the Cat. Elizabeth studied the picture of the feline celebrity and read the article below. Suddenly, she gave out a yell. "Rita! Rita! Come here!"

"I thought we weren't talking," Rita called back from across the aisle.

"Forget that," she ordered. "Come over here and read this!" She handed the paper to Rita. "Do I have a fantastic idea!"

"I don't get it," Rita said after she read the article. " 'Wanted, female cat to play opposite Clarence the Cat in a television commercial advertising Kitty Kat Cat Food.' "

" 'And she must like to play with can openers.' " Elizabeth pointed to the line.

"So what?" Rita asked.

"So what! How can you be so dense! This is the chance I've been waiting for all my life."

"Why? Are you a female cat with a hang-up on

can openers? You've flipped!" Rita started to twist the end of her thick braid, hoping to get it to turn under.

"Rita, listen. I have cats. In fact, I have five female, gorgeous, talented, photogenic cats!"

"Do they like can openers?" Rita asked sarcastically.

"You bet they will when I finish with them. Now, first things first. I've got to write a letter to this address and arrange for an audition."

"But don't the cats have to be professionals?"

"They won't know if they are or not. I'll sign the letter 'Ms. Elizabeth Dawson, Trainer and Manager of Exceptional Cats.' And we'll type the letter so that it looks professional. Let's meet at my house this afternoon. How about it?"

"Okay. But I think you're nuts. You'll never get an answer!"

"Want to make a bet?" Elizabeth said. Carefully, she tore the article out of the paper and put it in her jacket pocket.

Elizabeth's head was spinning with ideas. "Don't tell anyone about this article," she told Rita.

Her friend nodded.

Elizabeth knew she could trust Rita. They had been best friends since first grade. And Rita always kept a secret.

That afternoon they met at Elizabeth's house. After a quick snack, they went upstairs to the den.

"The first thing we have to do is write the

letter," Elizabeth said. "Then we have to teach my cats to like can openers."

Rita helped Elizabeth roll the big black typewriter on the stand out of the closet. They pulled it into the middle of the spare room and placed the desk chair beside it. Elizabeth flung herself on the faded green sofa bed.

"Will your mother mind if we use the typewriter?"

Elizabeth kicked her legs high into the air and let them land on the back of the sofa. "Anything goes in this room. My mother never fixed this place up because she planned to make it into a baby's room. Now, get some paper out of the second drawer of that desk and I'll dictate the letter."

"But I can't type!"

"Neither can I. You'll just go very slowly."

"Why don't you do it, Elizabeth?"

"Because I'm doing the thinking. And besides, you're the better speller. Now, roll the paper into the typewriter. You got it."

"It's coming out crooked!" Rita cried.

"All right, I'll help." Elizabeth went to the machine and carefully inserted a new sheet of paper.

"Why don't we write it out first and then I'll try to type it?" Rita suggested. "And I'll correct the spelling mistakes," she added smugly.

"That's the first good idea you've had. Get a pad and pencil. Top drawer desk." Elizabeth returned to the couch. "Dear Sir . . ."

"How do you know it's a sir?" Rita asked.

"Just write . . . Dear Sir. I have five female cats that would like to audition for the television commercial with Clarence."

"How do you spell audition?" Rita asked. "It hasn't been on our spelling lists."

Elizabeth dug into her dungaree pocket and pulled out the wrinkled newspaper article. "Copy it from here." She handed it to Rita. "Now, repeat it to me."

Rita flipped back her long braid of chestnut hair. Elizabeth watched with envy. When Rita wore her hair loose it was wavy and thick, almost to her waist. Elizabeth's was thin, without a single wave or curl.

Rita spoke slowly, mouthing each syllable carefully. "Dear Sir comma I capital letter have five female cats that would like to a-u-d-i-t-i-o-n for the television commercial with Clarence."

"Very good. Now add that they love can openers and Kitty Kat Cat Food."

"You can't say that! It isn't true."

"Believe me, it will be true when I finish with them."

"What if they hate Kitty Kat? They've never eaten anything but the brand your father's company makes."

"All cat food is alike. I've heard my father say so. He says it's only the packaging that's different. Besides, if they get hungry enough they'll eat."

"Well, I wouldn't be too sure."

"If it will make you happy, I'll buy some Kitty Kat and get them used to it."

"But your *father*, Elizabeth! What will he say if he sees another brand of cat food in the house?"

Elizabeth thought for a moment. "I'll just take the labels off. They look the same in the dish. Now keep writing, and sign it 'Yours truly, E. Dawson, Cat Trainer and Manager.' " Elizabeth looked over her friend's shoulder. "That looks good. Now, I'll round up the cats while you type the letter."

Elizabeth searched for nearly thirty minutes. She walked into her bedroom and found Princess Margaret on the bed, busily licking her long white hair. Cat was curled up on the dinette window sill, paws against the pane, sunning herself. Elizabeth found Ezmeralda spread out comfortably on Mr. Dawson's easy chair, taking a short nap, and Tinker Bell was cooling herself on top of the refrigerator.

One by one Elizabeth carried the cats into the den and then closed the door.

"That makes four," Elizabeth said to Rita. "I might as well give up on Snow Flake. She's so tiny. She must be up a drain pipe or something. How are you doing?" The beautiful Princess Margaret jumped on the couch and curled into a ball. Elizabeth went to the typewriter.

"That's terrible!" she yelled. "Look at all the X'd out letters and weird spacing. It sure doesn't look like my father's business letters."

"Well, I'm not a typist and you can just do it

yourself. I think it's a dumb idea, anyway. I bet you'll never get an answer."

"I bet I will, too, get an answer! Oh, no, Rita—the answer!" Elizabeth screamed. "It can't come here. My father will be furious if he sees letters from Kitty Kat. That's his number-one rival."

"I've been trying to tell you it won't work. Well, you could get the mail before he comes home."

"No good. It arrives while I'm in school. My mother goes through it first." Elizabeth smiled sweetly at her friend. "There's only one solution."

Rita looked at her blankly.

"We'll give *your* address."

"That's not so clever, Elizabeth, the name will be wrong."

"Then we'll put 'Elizabeth Dawson, Box Office SHAW.' That will look very businesslike."

"What about my mother?" Rita asked.

"Would she really notice? Seven people in your family—how can your mother keep track of all *that* mail?"

"Elizabeth, I have a feeling that you're going to get me into trouble." Rita pushed the machine away from her and suddenly the stand started to move—slowly at first, then it picked up speed. The girls watched helplessly. What a rickety noise it made as it rolled across the room until CRASH—right into an end table about eight feet from Rita's chair.

"Elizabeth!" Rita screamed. "Look!" The stand stopped when it hit the table but that didn't stop the typewriter. It kept moving, flying over the end table and then . . . THUD . . . it landed right on the floor, keys down.

"No!" The girls screamed.

"What is it?" Mrs. Dawson called from the bottom of the stairs. "Is anyone hurt?"

"No!" Elizabeth tried to sound calm.

In a few seconds Mrs. Dawson was standing in the doorway of the room. The four cats ran out. "Oh, my goodness! What is the typewriter doing there?" Mrs. Dawson pointed to the inverted machine.

"It was an accident, Mom."

"Accident! What kind of accident puts a twenty-pound typewriter upside down on the floor!"

Mrs. Dawson looked at Rita. She was still sitting in the chair in the middle of the room.

"I'm sorry, Mrs. Dawson. I was typing and it slipped!"

"Slipped! Typewriters don't slip! Rita, it's time you went home!"

Rita ran to the door. "I'm sorry . . . really I am. Goodbye, Mrs. Dawson." She gave a half wave to Elizabeth and dashed out the door.

"Why were you using your father's typewriter without permission?" Mrs. Dawson asked.

Elizabeth crossed her fingers behind her back. "We were just playing. I mean pretending. Rita was typing and I was giving her dictation." Elizabeth shifted from one foot to the other.

"A typewriter isn't a toy. It's an expensive piece of equipment." She bent down and tried to turn it over. "Give me a hand, Elizabeth." Together they pushed the machine upright. Mrs. Dawson tried the keys. They didn't move. "It's broken and I have no idea how much it will cost to repair. I swear, Elizabeth, every time you and Rita get together there's trouble. One day it's wanting to adopt a baby brother. So you two put signs up all over town: 'Elizabeth Dawson wants a brother. Call . . .' and *she* printed our telephone number! Then it's finding her tap dancing on my coffee table! And now this! I mean it, Elizabeth, why don't you play with Vivian for a change? Maybe you'll stay out of mischief."

"I hate Vivian."

"She seems like a nice, well-mannered girl. You should have something in common. At least ballet."

"Forget it. I'd rather be alone."

"Being alone is an excellent idea for now. Go to your room and stay there until I've talked with your father, young lady."

Elizabeth looked at the strange pile of machinery and started to feel her face turn hot. "I'm sorry, Mom," she said meekly.

"Sorry isn't going to change things. The typewriter is still broken. Now get moving," Mrs. Dawson said.

Elizabeth turned, headed out the door and into her room. There was a tap at her window as a small stone bounced off it. She opened the window and saw Rita on the back lawn looking up. Elizabeth could understand her pantomimed question.

"What is she going to do to you?"

"I don't know yet," Elizabeth called. "I have to stay in my room."

"For how long?" Rita gestured.

"Maybe till I've grown up!"

"She has to let you go to school. It's the law. Can I do anything for you?"

"Yes. I'm going to write the letter by hand. Come back in an hour and I'll drop it to you to mail. Oh, and bring me five cans of Kitty Kat Cat Food. I'll pay you back in school. Leave the cans behind the back-door steps."

"Okay. But I still think you're nuts."

Elizabeth watched her friend disappear into her own backyard. Then she turned and walked over to the desk. She took out a plain piece of white paper and a pen and printed in tiny letters: "Dear Sir." It looked too uneven. She tried another sheet and wrote in script. Again, the lines were not straight. *I've got to make it look like a business letter.* She took out her ruler. This time she guided each line. When she was finished, she admired her work. *This letter should get my cats an audition . . . I hope.*

14

2

ELIZABETH STUDIED THE DEGAS BAL-
lerina in the painting that hung on the wall across
from the foot of her bed. She wished she had a
soft billowing tutu to wear during ballet class that
would hide her chubby legs. Her leg extensions
never looked as good as Vivian's.

I'm not going to get out of bed today for
anyone, she thought. I'll die right here on top of
my blue quilt. People will come and view my
body dressed in dungarees and my Blunder Bread
polo shirt. My famous cats, stars of a million
television commercials, will surround me. And
my parents will weep. No visitors and no television for one whole week! What an unfair punishment for a little accident! They were wrong and
they'll admit it, after I die.

As image after image of consoling friend and
relative passed before her, Elizabeth felt better.

The only good that came from being home all week, Elizabeth thought, was being able to work with Tinker Bell, Ezmeralda, Snow Flake, Princess Margaret, and Cat. Each day at school Rita gave Elizabeth five cans of Kitty Kat Cat Food, and Elizabeth worked to prepare the cats for their audition. First she put a can opener in a bowl and then she added a little Kitty Kat. The first day Princess Margaret had walked to the bowl. Daintily she'd put one white paw into it and had pushed the can opener. She'd pulled her paw away, then put it back. Tinker Bell had quickly decided to join the game. One gray-striped paw and one white paw were now pushing the can opener around in the Kitty Kat Cat Food.

"No, no girls," Elizabeth had said. "I want you to taste the food too. Not just play!"

Princess Margaret and Tinker Bell had watched sadly as Elizabeth removed the can opener.

Cat had walked bravely up to the bowl and looked in. She'd sniffed. Her black tail had stiffened. Then she'd started to eat. As she ate, her tail had gotten higher and straighter. The four cats had watched. Then Ezmeralda and Snow Flake dashed for the bowl. They'd stopped, looked, and played with the food until they'd started to eat too. They really seemed to enjoy the new diet. In fact, by the end of the week they wouldn't touch the brand her father brought home from his office.

"Don't we need another case of food?" Mr. Dawson had asked at dinner one night.

"I don't understand it," Mrs. Dawson had said. "Someone in the neighborhood must be feeding the female cats!"

Elizabeth had said nothing. She'd wiggled a bit in her chair, trying to get her heart out of her stomach.

Mrs. Dawson's voice brought Elizabeth back to reality. "Breakfast!" she called.

"I'm not interested!" Elizabeth called back. She started to daydream again. *First, I'll change my name. Having a four-syllable name is a pain. I'll change it to something cute and perky like Wendy . . . Cindy . . . Sandy . . . Deedee.* She dragged herself to the full-length mirror on the closet door. *I look like a nothing,* she thought as she stared at her waistless body, uncombed reddish-brown hair, and bangs that almost touched her eyebrows. *What I need is a new face!* She took her brush off the dresser and started to brush her hair. She tried to part it on one side but the hair fell into her face. She pulled it back, but it made her look like a pumpkin. *Wait a second, I've got an idea. If I trim my hair, just a little, maybe my face will look thinner.* Elizabeth looked at the girl in the painting. *Now that's a great look!* She glanced at the ballerina again. *She looks very French. If I just trim my hair a tiny bit and blow dry it puffy, maybe I'll look French too!*

"Come down, Elizabeth," Mrs. Dawson called. "I have a job for you to do in the basement polishing some of my antique silver."

"But my punishment is over today!"

"Helping your mother isn't punishment."

"I'll be down later." Elizabeth heard the kitchen door close. Then she walked into her parents' bright pink bedroom. On the only windowless wall was her mother's vanity table. It had layers of pink flowered fabric around it that matched the curtains and bedspread. There were drawers on one side and a glass top. On the wall was a giant oval mirror. Elizabeth opened the second drawer. There were the long, thin scissors her mother used to trim her bangs. She sat down on the tufted pink velvet stool. She held a long clump of hair in her left hand. Her hand began to shake. Should I do it? She hesitated. Then she began to cut. It's *my* hair. Besides, my mother probably won't even notice. She cut about three inches from her scalp, dropping the bunch of hair into the wastepaper basket next to the table. She felt confident now. Carefully she held another cluster of hair and cut it off, leaving only about two inches. When she was finished she shook her head. Not bad, she thought, for a non-professional. It looks floppy and uneven like a shaggy dog, but I like it. She trimmed a little hair near each ear. Then she put the scissors back in the drawer and tried to brush the loose hair off the vanity top and stool. The right side seemed a little shorter than the left but it didn't matter. I look pretty good, Elizabeth thought. This is just what I need to cheer me up. Princess Margaret walked in and leaped on the dressing table. She stared at Elizabeth with her big green eyes.

"Do you like it?" The cat yawned and looked away. "Some pal you are! You're lucky. You were born beautiful. All you need is a lick here and there. In my next life I'm coming back as a cat!"

Elizabeth went to the hall bathroom and washed her hair quickly in the sink, using only a drop of shampoo. Two glasses of water rinsed the foam out. She vigorously towel-dried her wet head and then reached for the blower. In a few minutes her hair was dry and standing out at different angles like a porcupine's bristles.

She stood back and smiled at the new image in the mirror. She used her comb to bring wisps of hair onto her brow. The little tufts of hair around her face did seem to make it look less round.

Back in her room, Elizabeth stood in front of her own mirror and smiled again. She tucked in her shirt, took a wide leather belt out of the closet, and put it around her waist. Princess Margaret stared at her again.

"Well, how do I look?" Elizabeth asked the cat. Princess Margaret yawned.

I really look older, she thought. Maybe even old enough to get into a PG movie alone. Not bad at all.

A pebble tapped the window. Elizabeth looked out and saw Rita.

"Can you come out today?" Rita asked.

Elizabeth pushed the window up and stuck her head out.

"Is that you, Elizabeth?" Rita called.

Elizabeth nodded.

"You look different!"

"Different good or different bad?" Elizabeth asked.

"Just d-d-different. Everyone's going to notice you in school."

"Great! I'm on my way downstairs. Hey, was there anything in your mail?"

Rita shook her head from side to side.

"Stay there. I'll be right down." Elizabeth closed the window and took a last approving look in the mirror. She felt a little let down because an answer had not come from Kitty Kat. But she reminded herself that Rita mailed it only seven days ago. She marked each day off on her desk calendar.

Elizabeth raced down the stairs and pushed the kitchen door open. Her mother's back was to her. She was clearing the dishes from the table.

"You'll have to make your own break . . ." Her voice stopped as she turned to face Elizabeth. She froze. Her mouth opened and her eyebrows almost touched her hairline. "What have you done to yourself?" she screamed.

"Mother," Elizabeth said and smiled. "How do you like the new me?"

Mrs. Dawson sat down. She looked as if she'd faint. Then she finally found her voice. "What did you do to yourself?"

"I just trimmed my hair a little, that's all," Elizabeth answered. "I got tired of my old self. I want to be somebody new and different. I think I look great, don't you?" She turned from side to side, modeling her new hairdo.

"But we're taking you out to dinner tomorrow for your birthday and you look . . ." Mrs. Dawson's face grew tight with anger. Elizabeth knew that look instantly.

"I look very French. Don't you think so?" Elizabeth asked.

Mrs. Dawson continued to stare.

"I saw the girl in my painting and I liked her hair."

"That's no reason to butcher yourself," Mrs. Dawson said bitterly.

Elizabeth felt terrible. Her mother was trying to ruin everything. She had to get away as fast as possible.

"Can I go outside and speak to Rita?" she asked. Mrs. Dawson was already reaching for the phone.

"Yes, but don't go far. I'm going to make an appointment for you at my beauty parlor."

"No!" Elizabeth cried. "I like my hair. I look different. Rita thinks so too."

"Different is the right word! You definitely look different, but," Mrs. Dawson played with Elizabeth's hair as she talked, "I think Marcia will be able to do something with it. Let's hope so."

Elizabeth slammed the back door on her way out. She knew her mother hated the loud bang.

In less than ten minutes Mrs. Dawson had

Elizabeth on the way to the beauty parlor. She even treated her to a shampoo and rinse before the restyling. Usually, Elizabeth only got a quick cut.

Everyone at school made a big fuss over the new hair style. Elizabeth's friends said she looked like a kewpie doll, but others called her a shaggy dog. She liked the attention. Thank goodness Marcia couldn't make all the ends even, Elizabeth thought.

3

ELIZABETH WAS SMILING AS SHE HALF skipped, half walked home from the bus stop. Rita was absent today, so there was no one to share school gossip with on the way home. Elizabeth could daydream instead. First she tried to think of a name for her new birthday present. Maybe "Softie" . . . That's pretty, "Softie Dawson." Such a precious beige kitten. How could I have not wanted her! Elizabeth skipped a little faster.

I'm exactly one month into my thirteenth year, she thought. If I lived in China I'd be thirteen already. She remembered how Mrs. Snyder had carefully explained that a Chinese child was one on the day it was born because the baby was starting its first year of life. So, if anyone asks my age, Elizabeth thought, I'll say thirteen. Well, maybe I'll say almost thirteen.

She turned into her driveway and walked to the house. When she got to the back door, she took the key from under the mat and let herself in.

"Mother!" she called. There was no answer. Elizabeth noticed the note taped to the refrigerator door. She read it. " 'I'm selling in the basement. Pretend I'm not home. Set the table for dinner. Mom.' "

Tinker Bell ran to Elizabeth's foot and rolled over on her back. Elizabeth rubbed the little gray tiger cat. "You think you're a dog, Tinker Bell." The cat wiggled and purred softly. "I'm glad you're not a fraidy cat like Snow Flake and Cat." Just as Elizabeth went to the refrigerator, the phone rang. She picked it up.

"Elizabeth! Elizabeth!" Rita shouted. "It came. I've got a large fat white envelope addressed to *you!*"

"Wow!" She heard her own voice echo through the house. A cat ran across the room and took shelter on the top of the dinette breakfront. Even Tinker Bell looked for a secure corner and curled up tightly.

"Read it to me!" Elizabeth screamed.

"Just a second, I have to open it."

Elizabeth waited impatiently.

"Ready?" Rita asked.

"Read it! Read it!" Elizabeth demanded.

Dear Sir:
Thank you for your interest in auditioning your cat (cats) for Kitty Kat Cat Food. We

are enclosing an application. Kindly fill it out and return it with a picture of your cat (cats). You will be notified if we are interested in a personal interview.

We are also including a fifty-cent discount coupon for Kitty Kat Cat Food. It is Clarence's way of saying thank you for your interest.

Sincerely,
Adam Marks

Elizabeth started to jump up and down. "I'll be right over!" she yelled and hung up.

"What's all the racket?" Mrs. Dawson called from the bottom of the basement stairs. "I have important clients in the cellar so please be quiet!"

"Mother, I just got . . ." She stopped suddenly. I can't tell her, she thought. I've got to keep this a secret until everything is set. No use in looking for trouble now.

"Mom, I'm going to Rita's house," she called.

Elizabeth zipped out the door and through the yard. Rita was waiting. "Come up to my room. My sisters aren't here."

Elizabeth read the letter again. " 'A picture . . .' How will I get pictures of all five cats? Maybe I should just pick the best-looking one," she said. "And I'll need film. I think I'll use black and white because it's cheaper."

"Can I help you?" Rita asked.

"Sure. You can be my assistant. I don't want to

hurt your feelings, Rita, but I need a . . . a more professional photographer."

"I understand," Rita said. Elizabeth could see her friend was disappointed.

"I've got it!" Elizabeth became excited. "I'll ask Norman Kelly. When his parents visited last week they said he was into photography at school. And he only lives around the corner." She paused for a moment and rethought the idea. "But I haven't seen him since he went to junior high. Oh, well, I have nothing to lose. I'll give him a call after I read the forms."

The girls discussed the application and ate a bag of chips. There were five identical forms, each one a page long. There were questions about the owner—address, phone number, occupation—and questions about the cat—name, description, age, weight, length, and special abilities. "A cinch," Elizabeth said. She decided to continue using Rita's address but would give the Dawson telephone number.

"No problem," Rita said. "You were right about the mail. My mother never even noticed the letter."

"I'll take the forms with me and call Norman from home."

As soon as she got home, Elizabeth went to the phone in her parents' room. She looked up the Kelly number in the little leather-bound book her mother kept next to her side of the bed. The she dialed. A deep voice answered: "Hello."

"May I please speak to Norman?" Elizabeth asked.

"This is Norman," the husky voice answered.

"But you don't sound like Norman Kelly."

"Well, it *is* Norman Kelly and who are you?"

"It's Elizabeth Dawson. You know, your neighbor around the corner."

"Little Lizzie Dawson?" he asked.

"I'm twelve." Elizabeth hadn't heard that nickname in years. She used to hate it. Now "Lizzie" sounded cute, especially when Norman said it.

"Terrific. Call me back when you're fourteen," Norman said abruptly.

"Wait!" She was afraid he'd hang up. "Norman, could you do me a favor . . . a really big, important favor?"

"What kind of favor, Lizzie?"

"You're into photography, right?" She thought she heard him mumble "Yes." "Well, I need pictures of five of my cats?"

"Why?"

"It's a secret. Before I tell you, you must promise not to tell anyone."

"I don't have time to play games. Now tell me, what is it?"

"A . . . a contest. It's a pet contest. I overheard your parents telling my folks that you're always taking pictures. How about taking some of my cats? I'll pay for the film."

"Why the secret business?"

"Because the contest is for the Kitty Kat Cat Food Company and my father works for Purrfect. I don't want to upset him."

"So you're going behind his back. I get it."

"Norman! You won't tell!"

"Mmmm . . . but what's in it for me? What do I get if you win?"

"A . . . a . . . how about a cat! My father gave me a kitten for my birthday. She has beautiful long beige hair and is definitely part Angora. Instead of having her fixed, I'll let her have a litter and you can have your pick."

"What do I want a cat for? I have a dog! What do *you* get if you win this contest?"

"Swear you won't tell."

"Why should I tell anyone?"

"The winning cat gets to be in a television commercial with Clarence the Cat." She liked being able to tell the story to someone other than Rita.

"Hey, there should be a lot of money in that! "I'll tell you what. If I take the pictures and one of your cats wins I want a cut."

"How much?"

"Fifty-fifty, Lizzie."

"That's not fair. My cats do all the work. All you have to do is take their pictures."

"If you think it's so easy, you take the pictures. That's my offer. Take it or leave it."

"Okay. But that's only fifty-fifty on the first commerical. If they make lots of commercials they're mine."

"You drive a hard bargain, Lizzie, but I'll take it. I'll make up a contract for you to sign when we get together for the shooting. When do you want to start?"

"As soon as possible. Today?" Elizabeth asked.

"Can't. Have to wait till after school tomorrow. Bring the cats over to my house about four. I'll have the lights set up in my basement."

"When will the prints be ready?"

"First I'll make contact sheets so we can choose which shots we want to go with. I can work on it over the weekend. I do all my own developing and enlarging in the basement. Well, partner, we're in business. See you at four tomorrow." He hung up.

Elizabeth ran back into her room and sat at the desk. Norman really sounded as if he knew what to do. She had made the right choice. Now, to fill out the forms.

She printed the information neatly. After "Owner's Occupation" she wrote "Animal Trainer." Then came measuring the cats. Should I include the tail or not? She wondered. She used her mother's yellow tape measure and measured from nose to beginning of tail. Then she measured the tail. None of the cats would stand still so she measured them lying down. Snow Flake was impossible so Elizabeth just estimated her length. On the form she wrote the length with tail and length without tail. Weighing was easy. She weighed herself, then lifted each cat in her arms and weighed herself again. She subtracted the two weights. The cat's weight was the difference.

By dinner time, Elizabeth had finished the forms and lay exhausted on the bed. A few new scratches had been added to her arms. But it was worth it. Her cats were going to be stars. She just knew it!

4

"RITA, YOU'VE GOT TO HELP ME!" Elizabeth shouted into the phone. "I'm going to meet Norman in twenty minutes, and I can't find two cats! Please sneak out of the house!" she begged. "Sore throat! That's not such a big deal. Helping me find my cats won't make your throat worse . . . Some friend!" Elizabeth slammed down the telephone receiver.

A gray carrying box with a plastic top stood by the kitchen door. Faint meows were coming from the air holes. Tinker Bell was in a cardboard box. Her little striped head was peeking out.

A large brown carrying box was open. Elizabeth place it on the floor next to the three plastic bowls. Then she took a box of dry cat cereal from the closet and started shaking it vigorously.

"Come, Cat! Come, Ezmeralda! Time for a

treat! Don't you want to have your picture taken?"

There was the tinkle of a bell. A calico cat peeked out of the pantry closet.

"Come, Ezmeralda!" Elizabeth tried not to scare her. She continued to shake the box. The black, red, white, and orange cat walked cautiously into the kitchen.

"Good girl! Here's your treat."

Elizabeth poured food into an empty bowl. Ezmeralda walked to the bowl and started to nibble. Elizabeth bent down and petted her, then scooped her up and put the cat into the brown carrier. Ezmeralda curled up in a corner and stared at Elizabeth. Cat followed Ezmeralda. She was black with white paws and only half the size of her sister. She jumped into the carrier. "Good girl," Elizabeth said, and petted her. "I think you'd better join your sisters, Tinker Bell," Elizabeth said. She lifted the gray tiger cat out of the box, put her into the carrier, and closed the top. Tinker Bell protested with a loud meow.

"Now where are Snow Flake and Princess Margaret?" Elizabeth whispered to the cats. "If I know Snow Flake, she's probably hiding very close by, watching everything."

Elizabeth tiptoed around the kitchen. She opened all the cabinet doors and looked under the sink. "Where's your sister?" she asked the other cats. She looked on the top of the refrigerator. Then she went into the laundry area of the pantry. The front of the washing machine was open. Elizabeth bent down and put her hands into the round hole. She felt soft, smooth hair.

"Got you!" she called. Snow Flake wiggled and scratched, but Elizabeth pulled her out and held her. Quickly she put her into a gray carrier and closed the top so she couldn't escape.

Now for Princess Margaret. "Where are you?" Elizabeth looked around the room. There in her father's chair was Princess Margaret curled up in a tight ball. She completely ignored Elizabeth and all the commotion.

"You're the most beautiful cat I have, but you're a real pain!" she said as she quickly picked up Princess Margaret and put her into the box. Princess Margaret didn't react.

Elizabeth tried to lift the two cat carriers. "They weigh a ton!" she thought. "I'll never get them to Norman's house alone, and they won't fit on my bicycle. I could use a wagon. I've got it!"

She ran to the garage and pulled out a battered gray doll carriage. After she wheeled it close to the back door, Elizabeth dragged each box to the carriage and loaded up.

"Okay, Norman! Here we come . . . five beautiful cats, one broken doll carriage, and me!"

Elizabeth felt silly walking down the block to Norman's house, pushing her old doll carriage.

"What cha got?" asked Mary Ann. She was playing jacks on her porch when Elizabeth rolled by.

"Nothing but a bunch of cats," Elizabeth said. She held her head up and quickened her pace. Luckily no one else was outside. A few cars passed, but she didn't recognize the drivers or passengers. She sighed with relief when she finally reached the Kelly house and rang the bell.

"Who is it?" a deep voice asked.

"Me, Elizabeth. I mean, Lizzie Dawson with my cats."

"Bring them in," Norman said.

"I need help!" she called.

"Okay." A few seconds later, a tall, handsome boy was looking at her. She stared at him. He still had wavy blond hair but his freckles were gone and only one thin silver band remained on his teeth. He was wearing a pale-blue crew-neck polo shirt that just matched his eyes. And, she noticed, he didn't even have pimples!

Elizabeth couldn't talk. She felt a flash of heat. It was Norman Kelly all right, but he didn't look like the Norman that used to walk her to the bus stop when she was in kindergarten. Since he had left public grade school, she had only seen him passing in the car with his parents.

"I'm . . . L . . . L . . . Lizzie," she stammered.

"No kidding!"

"You don't look like Norman . . . I mean, you used to have a funny tooth that stuck out and sort of crossed over the other one." The minute she said that she wanted to bite her tongue and crawl into a hole.

Norman laughed. All his teeth showed. They were even. "My father will be happy to hear that all his money for braces wasn't wasted."

Elizabeth blushed. "You've grown a lot taller too."

"So have you." He smiled. Elizabeth liked his warm open grin.

"You just look so different.

"Well, it's me. Come on, I haven't got all day. Let's get to work!"

Each carried a box of meowing cats. The basement steps were directly across from the backdoor entrance.

"Hurry up! I want to get this over with."

He went first. The steps were narrow. Elizabeth was afraid she'd fall.

"I'll put on the light," Norman said. He pulled the string hanging at the bottom of the stairs.

The basement was unfinished. The walls were gray cement and the ceiling was crisscrossed with beams and pipes. The large room was cluttered with trunks, sleds, tools, and mounds of junk. Behind the stairs was a large water heater. One corner was partitioned off with old khaki blankets hung over ropes. A white sheet was laid out carefully on the floor with two floodlights standing at the edge. A 35-millimeter camera on a tripod was placed directly between the two lights.

"This is my office," Norman announced proudly, sweeping his arms wide to encompass the whole basement. "And that's my dark room."

He pointed to the blankets. "I plan to put up some plasterboard this summer." He walked further into the basement and lit two more overhead light bulbs. "Now, here's the contract." He took a piece of paper from an old battered desk and handed it to Elizabeth. Elizabeth started to read it.

"Here," he said and handed her a ballpoint pen.

"What's this mean: 'party of the first part retains the services of the party of the second part'?" she asked.

"A friend's brother is going to law school. He wrote it out, so it's all legal."

"But what does it *mean?*" she asked.

"You're the party of the first part. You sign your name there. I'm the second part," Norman explained. Elizabeth nodded. "The service is taking your cats' pictures and, in exchange, I'll receive fifty percent of the payment you receive from the first television commerical your cats do, *if* they get the job. Do you get it?"

Elizabeth nodded.

"Okay. Now sign here."

Carefully Elizabeth signed her full name. Then Norman bent down and wrote his name under hers. As his polo shirt rubbed against her bare arm, she felt the same funny, nervous feeling as when they met at the back door.

"Let's get to work," Norman said. "Put each cat on the sheet separately. I've got fast film so it doesn't matter if they move, but they have to stay on the sheet." He started adjusting the flood- lights.

Elizabeth decided to start with Tinker Bell. She was the most cooperative of the five cats. As soon as she opened the carrier, Ezmeralda, the calico cat, sprang out of the box. Cat stayed in the corner of the carrier, and Tinker Bell stood on her hind legs and looked out.

"Ezmeralda's escaped!" Elizabeth shouted. She picked up Tinker Bell and quickly closed the box.

"That's your problem, partner. Just bring me a cat," Norman said forcefully.

Elizabeth put Tinker Bell on the sheet. She was a perfect subject. Norman plugged in the lights and started to take pictures of her rolling around on the sheet.

"Terrific!" Norman said. "I'm getting some fabulous shots. This tiger cat's a natural. Get the next one ready."

"Ezmeralda! Where are you? She likes boxes," Elizabeth told Norman. He seemed more friendly now that he was behind the camera.

"Okay. I'll shoot her in a brown cardboard box. I'll aim down. Tinker Bell is finished."

Tinker Bell continued to play on the sheet. Just then, Elizabeth spied Ezmeralda going up the stairs.

"Help me catch her before she goes out the door!" she yelled to Norman. "She's cornered. I'll try to grab her, but if I miss, you be ready."

Together they trapped the calico cat. Elizabeth stroked her gently and placed her in the box. Norman was grinning when he returned to the camera.

"Get out of the picture, Lizzie!" he shouted.

"I'm afraid she'll run away again."

"Pet her, then pull back. Then pet her again. I'll count, and on the odd numbers you get out of the shots."

"*One* . . . two . . . *three* . . . four . . . *five* . . . six . . . *seven* . . . it's working! Good . . . good shot . . . nice!"

Norman continued shooting for almost ten minutes. Ezmeralda began to enjoy the attention and purred.

"Finished with that one, too. Two down and three to go!" Norman said.

Whenever Elizabeth wasn't chasing a cat, she watched Norman closely. She liked the way his hair fell over his ears and formed a little curl on the left side. She imagined him behind a movie camera giving orders to eager assistants. Maybe someday he would win an Academy Award for best director!

It was a long afternoon. Elizabeth held Snow Flake in her arms during her session. Cat played happily with toys stuffed with catnip while Norman photographed her. And Princess Margaret posed like royalty and yawned. Norman kept telling her how great the shots were.

"You should win! I took some fantastic shots!"

"When will they be ready?" Elizabeth asked.

"I want to send them off as soon as possible." She didn't want the day to end, but she did want to get the photographs as quickly as possible.

"I'll call you as soon as I get the contact sheets developed. We can decide together which ones to blow up. I'm free most of the weekend."

"Me too." Elizabeth said.

Norman helped her carry the cats to the doll carriage at the back door.

"I really appreciate your help," she said and flashed a big smile. Again she felt a funny, nervous feeling. She decided she liked the sensation.

"Sure," said Norman. "Anytime. Who knows? Your cats might make me a famous photographer someday."

Elizabeth suddenly didn't care how famous Norman might become. All she knew was from now on she was going to try to run into him as often as possible!

5

THAT NIGHT ELIZABETH DREAMED that Norman was walking her to school. He held her hand when they crossed the street. The next morning when she remembered the dream, she felt warm and good inside. During school Friday, she couldn't concentrate on her lessons. Every boy looked like Norman from the back. But when each turned around, she felt a surge of disappointment.

She hoped there would be a phone message from Norman when she got home, but there was none. The application forms lay under her desk blotter. The envelope was addressed and stamped.

The phone rang. She jumped up.

"I'll get it," she called, and raced to the phone in her parents' bedroom. "Who is it?" she asked breathlessly.

"Have you heard from *him?*" It was Rita.

"No, Rita, but it's dangerous to talk. My mother could pick up the phone."

"Doesn't she know anything?" Rita asked.

Elizabeth tried to make her voice sound breezy. "I'm having Norman take some pictures for my album. In fact, he asked *me* if he could use my cats for a photography assignment."

"I get it. Smart! When is he going to show you his assignment?"

"Sometime this weekend."

"I heard from my sister that he's gorgeous. She's in his French class."

"Oh, he's okay." Elizabeth tried to sound casual. "I hardly noticed. We've known each other for years. Our parents are best friends."

"Can I go with you?"

"I thought you had a sore throat," Elizabeth said.

"That was yesterday. My mother made me stay home from school today to be on the safe side."

"Okay. I'll call you if Norman phones before ballet class tomorrow. Otherwise, I'll meet you at Madame Rollin's."

"Super. Can't wait," Rita said and hung up.

No one called Elizabeth Friday night. She watched one repeat television show after another. She didn't even enjoy the ones she hadn't seen. The evening dragged on and on.

That night she dreamed about Norman again.

This time, they were going to a movie together.

Saturday morning, she woke up full of confidence. She was certain he would call today and they would meet that night. Norman would be her first Saturday night date!

The morning was endless. She fed the male cats Purrfect Cat Food, but put Kitty Kat Cat Food in a separate bowl near the back door. Tinker Bell went to it immediately and the other female cats followed. She was careful to feed them when her parents weren't around.

No one called. She tried to read the paper, but couldn't concentrate. Finally she noticed her father's calculator on his desk and tried to figure out how many kittens her female cats would have had if they hadn't been fixed. If her oldest, Cat, had had two litters each year for ten years, and there were five kittens in each, she would have had a hundred cats. Tinker Bell was only five years old, so that would be fifty kittens, and Snow Flake was four, which made forty cats. And if their kittens started to have kittens? That would add up to thousands of cats!

Her stomach told her it was lunch time. She made herself a peanut butter sandwich. Then she picked up her dance bag and started for Madame Rollin's. Rita never walked with her because she had a piano lesson first.

When Elizabeth arrived at ballet school, the dressing room was already filled with young dancers. She really didn't feel like dancing today.

She'd rather have stayed home and waited for Norman's call. She hung her polo coat on a hook and started to unpack her ballet bag.

"I brought the tape," Vivian said. "There's no way to cheat!"

Slowly Elizabeth turned around. She squinted her eyes and pulled her lips tight and tried to look mean. They had been arch enemies since first grade. It had all started when Elizabeth had gotten the starring role in the Christmas play, and Vivian was picked for the lead in the annual dance recital.

"I'm thirty-seven inches long," Vivian announced. Carefully she bent down and put the metal tape measure at the inside arch of her black ballet slipper. Delicately she pulled the tape measure out of its silver container. It uncoiled up the inside of her thin, straight leg. "See," she said proudly, "my legs are now thirty-seven inches long, and I'm only eleven years old. *I* have the longest legs in the class." She bent her leg at the knee and did an extension which almost knocked Elizabeth over.

"Spiders have long legs too, but that doesn't make them dancers," Elizabeth said.

"You're just jealous," Vivian taunted.

"Ballet is in the heart." She turned away and started to pull her tights on. Out of the corner of her eye, she could see Vivian holding the tape measure. She wished she was with Norman and not at this dumb ballet class.

"Your turn next, Elizabeth," Vivian said.

"I've never heard of a dancer with short, stubby legs." Vivian bent down and started to measure Elizabeth's leg.

"I'm not interested in your game," Elizabeth said. She kicked her leg free and grabbed the tape measure.

Vivian turned her back and started walking. "You've got to face the truth, Elizabeth."

Elizabeth clutched the tape measure and threw it across the room. Unfortunately, it hit Patsy Keller smack in the back of the head.

"AAHHHH!" came a blood-curdling scream. "I've been shot!" Patsy started sobbing and taking deep, dramatic breaths. "Is there blood?"

"It was just a tape measure with a little metal tip," Elizabeth told her. By then, a crowd of girls had circled around the injured Patsy.

"What eez happening?" Madame Rollin demanded as she opened the classroom door. She was a thin woman with a strong dancer's body. Her wrinkled face and cold blue eyes stared into the crowd of students. "It eez too noizee. What eez de cause?" she demanded in her thick French accent.

Patsy continued to sob. Vivian stepped forward and did a little ballet curtsey. "Elizabeth hit Patsy on the head."

Madam Rollin looked at Patsy.

"It was just a tape measure. I . . . I mean I didn't mean to hit Patsy. I wanted to hit Vivian." Elizabeth mumbled.

"Out!" Madame Rollin said in a low angry

voice. "These things never happen in my country."

"But let me explain . . . please!" Elizabeth begged.

"Out! You are to go home . . . now! I will call your mama tonight."

Elizabeth grabbed her belongings and ran into the bathroom and started to sob. "I'll get even with her," she cried. She splashed water on her face.

"Elizabeth, are you okay?" A voice called from the other side of the bathroom door. "It's me, Rita."

Elizabeth unlocked the door and let her friend in.

"I heard what happened. Why did you throw the tape measure at Patsy?"

"I didn't throw it at her. I threw it at Vivian! Patsy just got in the way." Elizabeth pulled her dungarees on over her tights and tossed her slippers into the bag. "I don't have much time before class. I've got to get even with her. I want you to be my lookout, Rita. Let me know if anyone is coming."

"What are you going to do?"

"I'm not sure. But first I'm going to make everyone think I've left. Follow me."

They went back into the dressing room. Everyone was ready for class. The five-minute warning bell had just rung. Elizabeth went over to Patsy, who was now busy measuring her leg.

"I just wanted to apologize," Elizabeth said to Patsy. "It was an accident." Patsy didn't look up. "Come on, Patsy, you know I didn't mean to hit you. The tape was meant for Vivian."

"Well . . . okay." She looked at Elizabeth. "You could have killed me!"

"Friends?" Elizabeth said and smiled.

"Well, okay," Patsy said again and returned the smile.

Elizabeth put on her jacket and buttoned the toggles on the front. "Well, goodbye girls, I'll see you next Saturday, I hope!"

Rita walked with her to the reception area. "Goodbye, Rita." She pretended to go out the main door, but instead she slipped into the coat closet.

It seemed like forever, but finally she heard an "all clear!" Quickly she dashed into the dressing room. She passed two women talking in the reception area, but they didn't notice her. She closed the door to the dressing room and walked to the corner. There on the bench was Vivian's new round pink ballet bag. Quickly Elizabeth zipped it up. She took the bag and walked out the door, trying to look as casual as possible.

When she got to the stairs, Elizabeth started running. She looked back over her shoulder, but no one was following her. She stopped at the street corner and thought, what do I do now? I have only forty-five minutes left to do a job on Vivian!

She started to walk down the side street which led to the main shopping center in Edge Valley. She swung Vivian's bag as she walked. *If I had my magic markers, I could write everyone's name all over the bag, but I'd have to buy her a new bag.* Then she saw the pet shop.

That's it! And I don't need any money either! She ran into the small store. The little bell over the door tinkled. For a second she was overwhelmed by the odor.

"Elizabeth Dawson," Mr. Pete called from behind a pile of puppy cages. He was tearing up strips of newspaper and putting them into a bottom cage.

"My mother said I could have one after all, Mr. Pete," Elizabeth said and flashed her biggest grin.

"Why, that's marvelous, Elizabeth! I just can't stand the idea of putting the little ones to death, but giving them away has been hard." He straightened up and went into the back of the store. A moment later, he came back with a shoe box with an air hole punched in the top. "Do you have a place to put him?" he asked.

"Yes. Don't worry, Mr. Pete. He's going to get a lot of attention."

"Now don't open the box until you're ready to transfer him. He's a slippery little thing."

"Okay. Thank you. Thank you very much, Mr. Pete."

Elizabeth walked back to the school. In her right hand she held the shoe box, giving it extra support with her body. In her left hand she swung the pink bag. When she arrived at the ballet school's building, she went behind the stairwell. She knelt down and unzipped the ballet bag. Then she tilted the shoe box into the bag and opened the top a few inches. Gently she coaxed the occupant into the ballet bag, then quickly zipped it up, leaving a tiny space for air. She left the shoe box under the stairs and started up the steps.

The dressing room was now filled with younger girls and a few boys waiting for the three o'clock class to begin. It was a very noisy group, so no one paid much attention to Elizabeth as she put the pink bag on the bench exactly where Vivian had left it. When the warning bell rang, Elizabeth left the dressing room and slipped back into the front closet.

The classroom door opened. There was a great deal of chattering as Elizabeth's class shook Madame Rollin's hand and headed for the water fountain. Then the next class entered the room. Finally, the noise died down, and Elizabeth could hear only the low hum of voices. She felt her own heart beating. Her mouth became dry as she waited.

Suddenly, she heard the scream. It was the loudest scream she had ever heard. Then other screams joined it. Someone must have pulled the fire alarm because now the howl of the fire alert joined the chorus of screams and screeches.

I'd better get out of here, Elizabeth thought.

Just then, she heard the first word coming from the dressing room. "SNAKE!"

6

ELIZABETH CROSSED HER FRONT LAWN
and circled into the driveway leading to the back
door. She heard the telephone ringing. Her heart
suddenly began to pound. Was it Norman? She
ran to the back door.

"Is it for me?" she yelled into the house. She
jerked the screen door open, then let it slam
behind her. The ringing stopped.

"Mom, I'm here. Is the call for me?" Still no
answer. Then she heard movement upstairs. Elizabeth went to the foot of the stairs and called
again. Her mother appeared at the top of the
staircase.

"What happened today at ballet class, Elizabeth?"

All at once, Elizabeth knew who had just
called.

"Nothing happened. Why?" Elizabeth asked.

"Did you hit Patsy Keller with a tape
measure?"

"Yeh, but it was an accident. Mom, did I get any calls?"

Her mother walked slowly down the stairs. Elizabeth could tell from the expression on her face that a change of topic wasn't going to work.

"You're too old to throw things at people."

"Mom, I was just returning Vivian's tape measure, and Patsy's head got in the way."

"Keep talking," Mrs. Dawson said. Her blue eyes stared directly into Elizabeth's. "Vivian found a snake in her ballet bag."

"No!" Elizabeth said. She tried to sound surprised.

"Yes! In her new pink ballet bag." Her mother paused for a moment. "Did *you* put it there?"

Elizabeth was silent. She turned away. Tears started to fill her eyes. She was caught.

"Okay," Mrs. Dawson said. She put her arms firmly around her daughter. "Let's sit down in the living room and talk this out."

Elizabeth sat next to her mother on the plush couch. Tears began rolling down her cheeks.

"Vivian is mean and spiteful. And . . ." Elizabeth found it difficult to speak between her sobs. "I . . . I hate her."

"That's a terrible thing to say about a girl. What has she done to you, Elizabeth?"

"She's always bragging about being a better dancer and having longer legs."

"She *does* have longer legs." Mrs. Dawson said.

"I know, but you can be a good dancer with

short legs, too. She wanted me to measure my legs with a tape measure!"

"Then what happened?"

"I threw the tape measure and Patsy got in the way. I hit her by accident. Honest."

"Was she hurt?"

"No, not really, but Madame Rollin made me leave class."

"And that's when you decided to get even," her mother added.

Elizabeth nodded. "And I got caught. No matter what anyone else does, I always get caught," she cried.

"Elizabeth, you look for trouble, it never looks for you. You should have ignored Vivian." Elizabeth nodded. "I want you to do two things. First, apologize to Madame Rollin when you pick up that reptile, and then tell Vivian you're sorry."

"I don't ever want to speak to Vivian again!"

"Elizabeth, you gave the girl a bad scare. She was wrong to tease you, but you were wrong to frighten her. The least you can do is say you're sorry."

"But . . ."

"Do what I say—and don't you dare bring that snake here!" Mrs. Dawson said. As Elizabeth started for the stairs, Mrs. Dawson added, "Oh, by the way, Norman Kelly called. I wonder what he wants?"

Elizabeth suddenly lit up. The tears dried in a flash and a broad grin spread across her face.

"Er . . . beats me! I'll call him back right now."
She started for the phone.

Her mother gave her a questioning look. "Remember, Elizabeth, you've got to do what I asked before you make any other plans for this weekend."

"Sure. I'll call Vivian, after I call Norman back. Then I'll go to ballet school and get the snake." She started running up the stairs.

"Don't forget to take a shoe box!" Mrs. Dawson called as Elizabeth disappeared into the master bedroom.

Elizabeth ran to the phone next to the bed and quickly dialed the Kelly number from memory. Norman answered.

"Norman?" she asked.

"Yeh, it's me."

"Lizzie . . . " Elizabeth decided she'd be Lizzie for Norman only. "How did the pictures turn out?"

"Fantastic. I really had my doubts when we started, but these pictures are good, partner. Get over here immediately!"

"I've got to do something first, but I'll be over in an hour. By the way, can my best friend, Rita, come?"

"I don't care as long as she doesn't yap a lot. I hate chattering girls."

"Terrific. See ya, Norman." Quickly she looked up Vivian's number and dialed. Vivian answered.

Elizabeth swallowed before she spoke. "Vivian," Elizabeth blurted out, "I'm sorry I put the snake in your ballet bag."

"You should be sorry. That horrible thing is still in my ballet bag. I wouldn't touch it for a million dollars! You're awful, Elizabeth. Really sick!" she shouted.

"You're no angel either. Where's the dumb bag? I'll get rid of the snake. It's only a baby, you know. It can't hurt you."

"It's ugly. I left it in Madame Rollin's office."

"I'll go over and get it."

"I hope Madame Rollin kicks you out of ballet school and the recital," Vivian singsonged into the phone.

"You're the worst!" Elizabeth snapped and hung up.

Next she called Rita and told her to get over to Norman's house in one hour.

"What are you going to wear?" her friend asked.

"Clothes!" Elizabeth said impatiently.

"You mean you're not going to put on anything special for him?"

"Knock it off, Rita. I've got other problems now, like a date with a snake. I'll meet you. Bye."

She grumbled with impatience as she walked past her mother's vanity mirror. She glanced quickly at herself. Maybe I'll put on a different T-shirt. She tugged it down and smoothed out the wrinkles on the picture of the television star. Noticing her mother's hairbrush she took it and brushed her hair vigorously. Then she shook her head. The uneven ends puffed out and fell into soft wisps framing her round face. She smiled at the reflection. She looked thinner too. Maybe all the excitement was making her lose weight. She surely hoped so. Running down the stairs, she called, "I talked to Vivian, Mom. Now I'm off to pick up that little bitsy baby snake and apologize to Madame Rollin for disturbing class."

"Good girl, and take the shoe box in the hall closet," Mrs. Dawson called from the kitchen. She seemed pleased. "I'm certain everything will work out, Elizabeth."

Elizabeth grabbed the multicolored rectangular box from the closet floor. "I'm meeting Rita afterward."

"Okay, but why did Norman Kelly call?" Mrs. Dawson asked through the kitchen door.

"Oh, nothing important. He took some pictures of my cats and he wants to show them to me."

Elizabeth heard the door swing open. Her mother's head poked out of the doorway. "That's nice, dear. I didn't know you two were friendly. Nice family."

"See you later, Mom." She gave a half wave and opened the door. She paused for a second, then decided to use the front door as an exit for a change.

As she walked toward the ballet school, she thought about her future. It won't be long now before the pictures will be in the mail and my cats will be on their way to stardom. She held the shoe box tightly. Oh darn! What am I going to do with the snake?

7

"*Bonjour,* MADAME ROLLIN," ELIZA-
beth said almost in a whisper as she entered the
ballet teacher's small partitioned office. Madame
looked up and did not give her usual friendly
hello.

"Elizabeth!" she said and indicated to the
chair.

Elizabeth sat down. "*Bonjour,*" she repeated.
She felt so silly using the French words Madame
insisted upon. *Bonjour, oui,* and *merci* were supposed to bring culture into her life. Even if she
couldn't speak any other words in the language.
Well, it impressed her mother.

Madame Rollin continued to frown. Every
wrinkle looked like a heavy pencil mark. Elizabeth had never sat so close to her teacher. She
could see little gray specks at the roots of her jet-
black hair which was pulled into a tight bun at the
nape of her neck.

"What do you have to say?" She stared coldly at Elizabeth.

"I'm sorry . . . about today."

Madame did not respond.

"It was all an accident. I mean with Patsy and the tape measure."

Still no response.

"Vivian was bugging me . . . about my legs."

Not even a blink from Madame.

"She said her legs were longer than mine."

Madame nodded. "Zes eez truth."

Elizabeth slumped into the chair. "But it was the way she did it . . . measuring with a tape measure and all that."

"Up! Up!" Madame pointed to Elizabeth's back. "Alwaz must be straight." Elizabeth stiffened. "Maybe the dance eez not for you."

"No! Please, please! I want to dance! I love coming to ballet class. I'll never do anything like this again."

"All right, Elizabeth. We will see. But I do not know if you may continue next year. It eez up to you."

"Thank you . . . I mean *merci, merci* very much."

"Now get theez thing out of Vivian's bag and out of here!" She turned her head toward the back wall and lowered her eyes to Vivian's pink ballet bag.

"Yes, *oui!* I brought a shoe box." Elizabeth darted to the bag and unzipped it. Without look-

ing she groped around till she felt the smooth body. "Got him!" She saw Madame turn away. She put the tiny gray reptile into the shoe box and closed the top. "All done," she said.

"Out! Out with it!" Madame said sharply.

Elizabeth left quickly, carrying the box under her arm. "Goodbye, Madame. I'll see you next Saturday."

"Mademoiselle Elizabeth, *au revoir*."

Elizabeth noticed that her teacher still did not smile.

The reception room was empty. The last class had finished at four. Elizabeth sat down on a cigarette-scarred couch and tried to figure out her next move. She found a hair clip in her pocket and punched two air holes in the top of the box. "Poor little fellow. If I take you back to Mr. Pete's he'll probably have to put you to sleep. Besides I did promise to give you a home. Mine is out. Maybe I should just let you go in some woods. Hey, maybe Rita or Norman might have some ideas. Wait a second. I've got a brainstorm." She jumped up and raced out of the school.

Two blocks away Elizabeth saw a stationery store. The more she thought about her plan, the more it excited her. She went in, made three purchases, and left.

Rita was waiting in front of Norman's house. Elizabeth stared at her and couldn't believe her own eyes!

"I didn't know you owned pantyhose and

heels!" Elizabeth said. Perhaps she's going out to dinner, Elizabeth thought.

"I got them when I was a bridesmaid at my cousin's wedding. They make me look older, don't you think?" Rita asked.

"Maybe older, but definitely stupid! A denim skirt and yellow shoes!"

Rita stopped smiling. "Really bad?" she asked.

"If I were you, I'd hide them behind a bush and go inside barefoot." Rita kicked off the shoes.

"Who's the gift for?" Rita asked as she rolled down the pantyhose.

"I'm not sure."

"That doesn't make sense. Why did you buy it?"

"I didn't buy it. I wrapped it. It's easier to give something away when it's a present."

Rita stuffed the pantyhose into one of her shoes and hid them behind a large evergreen bush on the Kelly's lawn. "Doesn't make sense to me."

"Forget it. You look normal now. Let's go."

Elizabeth rang the back doorbell. This time Norman greeted her with a warm smile.

"This is my friend Rita."

"Hi! Come on in." The girls followed Norman down the basement stairs. "It must be warm today if you're going barefoot already."

"Yes. I always go barefoot. I hate shoes." Rita said quickly.

Elizabeth stayed right behind Norman. She thought she caught a whiff of aftershave lotion. "Can't wait to see the pictures."

"These are just the contact sheets. We have to choose from them, remember. Come over to the table." Both girls followed him.

On top of an old bridge table were sheets of stiff paper. Some were curling at the edges. The girls stared down at the scattered sheets. Elizabeth could see only little rows of black and white squares.

"Here, use this!" Norman handed her a large magnifying glass. She held the black handle and tried to focus on a tiny square.

"That's Ezmeralda in the box!" Elizabeth shouted excitedly. "And there are dozens! Look!"

"Here's a red pencil. Now you mark the ones you like the best."

"I like them all!" Elizabeth could hardly believe her eyes. There were hundreds of tiny snapshots of her beautiful cats. Row after row passed under the magnifying glass, like a reel of motion picture film. "How can I possibly choose?"

"Just concentrate on one pose at a time. Then we'll narrow it down to which pose is the best of each cat."

"Norman, you're fabulous!" Elizabeth felt like kissing him or at least throwing her arms around him.

"Thanks. I personally like the picture of you with Snow Flake. You know, you're very photogenic."

Elizabeth couldn't believe her ears. She mumbled a quick thank you and Rita gave her an admiring smile.

"Look, this is going to take some time so why don't you two sit down here and get to work."

Elizabeth studied each frame carefully, deciding how much she liked each one. Norman agreed or disagreed with her choices. Sometimes he would take out a blue pencil and put lines around the picture. "That's called cropping," he said.

"Look at this picture of Tinker Bell wriggling on her back!" Rita screeched, jumping up and down wildly. "You're going to win. I just know it."

Norman frowned. Elizabeth picked up the cue. "Rita, calm down."

The three of them continued to examine each little frame.

"I'm getting hungry," Rita said. "What time is it?"

Norman looked at the old kitchen clock he had hanging by a nail on the wall. "Seven-fifteen."

"Oh, no! I'm late for dinner!" Rita cried. "I'll get killed."

"Me too," Elizabeth said unhappily. "But I can't quit now. You go, Rita, and I'll finish up."

"Okay, but you'd better call your mother, Elizabeth." Rita started to leave. "The pictures are great, Norman. Anytime you need a model I can bring my parakeet over." She disappeared up the stairs.

"What a kid," Norman said with disgust.

"Look, Lizzie, why don't you give your mother a ring and tell her you're eating here. I'll make some sandwiches and we can finish up tonight. Tomorrow I'll make the blow-ups."

"Terrific. But aren't your parents coming home?"

"Never see them on Saturday nights. They always have dinner dates. Don't worry, I won't poison you. I grill a neat cheese sandwich and there are Cokes in the fridge."

"Sounds terrific, Norman." Elizabeth was thrilled. She was having her first date, and a *dinner* date no less. She was sure her mother wouldn't object. After all, they were close friends of the Kellys, and her mother had said he came from a nice family.

"Where's the phone?" She smiled broadly at Norman.

"On the wall in the kitchen." She started toward the stairs. Then she saw the package neatly wrapped in flowered paper with yellow ribbon around it. In one corner she had pierced two small holes. She hesitated. Should she take a chance and give the box to Norman? Why not? He wasn't a sissy. Besides, she had nothing to lose. If he didn't like it she could say it was only a joke and give it to someone else. She grabbed the box.

"Norman! I almost forgot. I brought you a surprise. Here." She handed him the brightly wrapped shoe box.

He looked up. His eyes brightened. She adored the way he looked at her. "Yeh? Pass it over." Elizabeth followed his command. "Thanks, Lizzie," he said as he started to unwrap the box.

Elizabeth held her breath. Would he like it?

"It's a baby garter snake!" Norman said. He looked down into the box and beamed. Without hesitating, he touched the snake gently.

Suddenly she felt funny pangs in her stomach, like when she was on a roller coaster. "It's called a Dekay snake and it will grow only ten to sixteen inches long." Elizabeth recited what Mr. Pete had told her. "He eats earthworms and small insects."

"Lizzie, this is a super gift. I can't wait to take pictures of old D K when he's shedding his skin." He flashed a broad grin.

"I was sure you'd love it." Elizabeth beamed the whole way up the stairs. She picked up the kitchen telephone and dialed automatically. Her mother answered.

"Hello," Mrs. Dawson said.

"Mom, it's me . . . Elizabeth."

"Where are you?" she said angrily.

"At Norman Kelly's house."

"What are you doing there?"

"Norman was showing us the pictures he took of some of my cats and we forgot what time it was."

"Elizabeth, you've been very inconsiderate. It's almost seven-thirty. Your father and I have been very worried. Thank goodness Rita's mother called asking for her daughter. We realized you both must be together."

"I'm sorry, Mom. Listen can I stay here a little longer? We're just finishing up."

"What about dinner? Your father and I are going out."

"I'll grab something here."

"Well, I don't know," her mother said.

"Please, Mom. We're deciding which pictures are best!"

"Oh, all right. But be home no later than nine."

"Yes. Thanks." Elizabeth put down the receiver and turned to Norman. "I can stay till nine."

"Great." He was generously buttering four pieces of white bread.

"Can I help?" Elizabeth asked. He nodded and they worked side by side at the narrow butcher-block counter next to the stove. At first they talked generally about the cats. Elizabeth tried to recite each cat's year of birth. "Did Butch come before King Arthur or after?" she questioned herself.

"Bet you can't tell one cat from the other." Norman chuckled as he spoke. He flipped the sandwiches like flapjacks and almost missed the frying pan. They laughed.

"Yes I can." Elizabeth felt herself blush. He was teasing her. "If you lined up all the cats in the world, I bet I could pick out my twelve cats and that includes my kitten, Softie."

"I think the sandwiches are done," Norman said.

Elizabeth was so hungry by now that she eagerly reached across the table and picked up one of the grilled cheese sandwiches.

"Ouch!" she yelled, dropping the sandwich as though it were a hot coal.

Norman looked startled. "What's wrong?" he asked.

"I burned my hand," Elizabeth moaned. She shook it vigorously trying to ease the pain. It didn't help.

Norman leaned across the table and took Elizabeth's hand very tenderly.

"I'm sorry," Norman said. "The sandwiches just came off the stove. You should have known it was hot."

Elizabeth did not take Norman's remark as a reprimand. All she heard was the deep concern in his voice. She forgot the argument. All she knew was that Norman was caressing her hand, and she wanted it to go on forever. That wonderful warm feeling filled her body again.

"Let's run some cold water over your hand," Norman suggested. "That will help the pain."

They went to the kitchen sink and Norman turned on the cold water. Elizabeth let the water pour over her hand and she began to smile.

"It really does help," she said. "It feels better already."

They returned to the table and began to eat their dinner. For a little while there was an uncomfortable pause while they finished their sandwiches. Was the magic over? Norman asked a few questions about his old teachers from grade school and Elizabeth answered politely. They cleaned the kitchen together. Elizabeth watched as Norman put the dishes and utensils away. He was very careful and stacked everything neatly. Then they went back downstairs to finish choosing cat pictures.

Elizabeth checked the time. It was nearly nine o'clock. Her first date with Norman was over and she had almost ruined it by burning her hand. Maybe he thought she was dumb!

"Lizzie," Norman said at the back door. "I had fun tonight, I really did. When you asked me to photograph your cats, I thought it would be a drag, but I was wrong."

"Gee, Norman, I'm glad. I had a good time too."

"Good night, Lizzie," Norman said affectionately.

"Thanks for dinner."

"See you soon."

Elizabeth felt like skipping all the way home. He did have a good time! With every step she took she sang to herself, Lizzie, Lizzie, Lizzie. She smiled at the sound of it. It's the most wonderful name in the world . . . next to Norman!

8

THE NEXT DAY THE BLOW-UPS OF THE cats were ready. When Elizabeth went to pick them up, Mrs. Kelly greeted her at the front door.

"Elizabeth, how nice to see you," she said, extending her hand as she smiled warmly. Elizabeth returned the gentle handshake. "Norman left this envelope for you. He's at baseball practice."

Elizabeth sighed. She couldn't imagine why he had decided to play ball, after working with her last night.

"Elizabeth, why such a sad face?"

Elizabeth blushed from embarrassment. Could Mrs. Kelly know from her face how she felt about Norman?

"Cheer up, Elizabeth. The pictures are quite good." Mrs. Kelly handed her the large tan envelope.

"Thank you, Mrs. Kelly." She tried to force a smile.

She could hear the front door close as she walked away from the house. "Damn it!" she said under her breath. She felt like crying. And really, she thought, it was a silly thing to want to cry about. After all, she'd have plenty of chances to be with Norman again. It was only one day out of a lifetime.

When Elizabeth turned the corner into her block, there was Mary Ann playing jacks on her porch.

"I challenge you!" Mary Ann called.

"Not today. I've got some business to take care of."

"You know, Elizabeth, since you've been seeing Norman you've become too busy for everyone. What are you two up to?"

"None of your business!" Elizabeth quickened her pace.

"Secret! Secret! Elizabeth has a secret!" Mary Ann shouted. "Oh, shut up!" Elizabeth ran the last few steps to her house and rounded the corner of the lawn. She didn't stop to catch her breath until she reached the back door. She sat down on the back steps and looked around. She was alone. She stared at the tan envelope for a moment, then pulled the little metal butterfly tab together to release the flap. Carefully, she pulled the glossy 8 × 10s out. A magnificent white, long-haired cat stared at her. Princess Margaret was gorgeous. Unbelievably beautiful! Next, was a photo of Ezmeralda peeking out of a box. And there she was, Elizabeth, with Snow Flake on her lap. She was looking at the cat. Their eyes met and seemed to be saying something to each other. Cat was playing with a toy mouse between her paws and Tinker Bell was in a somersault position trying to catch her tail.

Elizabeth could hardly keep from jumping up and down. Behind the last loose photograph was a second group of pictures clipped together with a handwritten note attached. The script was bold and written in blue magic marker. It read, "This set is for you. Call me as soon as you hear from Kitty Kat. Your partner, Norm."

A letter from Norman! She would keep it always. She put the pictures back into the envelope and pushed open the back door. Her heart was pounding. She took giant leaps across the kitchen floor, then did spins to the bottom of the stairs. As she started up the steps, she sang a nonsense melody in a falsetto voice. She slammed the door to her bedroom and threw herself onto the bed.

"I'm going to win! I just know it!" She cuddled the envelope in her arms. Then she swung her legs up into the air and began to sing again. The sound of a car made her freeze.

Oh! My parents! She started to push the envelope under the desk blotter. She stopped. They can see the duplicate set. After all, she had told her mother on the phone that Norman was taking pictures of her cats.

Tomorrow I'll mail the application with the pictures. And maybe by this time next week, I'll be the owner of a famous feline personality.

9

"YOU GOT A LETTER! YOU GOT A LET-
ter!" Rita shouted breathlessly, as she burst into
the Dawson kitchen. She handed the envelope to
Elizabeth.

Nine days had passed since Elizabeth mailed
the five applications and five photographs. Her
heart pounded. This was it. The return address
was Cunningham, Anderson, Tate and Schwartz
Advertising Agency, 550 Madison Avenue, New
York. Good thing her mother wasn't home.

"Open it!" Rita demanded.

Elizabeth stared at the white rectangle. It was
regular letter size. Was that a good sign? She felt
disappointed. It was too small to contain con-
tracts or important papers.

"Elizabeth, what's wrong with you? Open it!
I'm dying to hear what's inside."

"Don't rush me, Rita. This could be the most important letter of my life. It could be the beginning of my professional career—or the end of it."

Elizabeth sat down at the table. She held the envelope. It was light. The outline of the folded paper inside was visible. She took a deep breath, then opened it slowly, tearing along the V-shaped back flap. Pulling the sheet out, she took a few more deep breaths. Carefully, she unfolded the paper and began to read. Rita leaned over and read the letter with her.

Elizabeth's eyes widened. Her mouth opened as she focused on the typewritten words. "I don't believe it!" she said.

"Wow! Fantastic!" Rita said.

"I've got to call Norman!" Elizabeth said excitedly. Clutching the paper in her hand, she ran to the wall phone and started to dial. Her heart was going thump, thump, thump. It was all she could do to keep from jumping up and down.

"Hello, Norman, this is Lizzie. Guess what?" She didn't wait for him to answer. "They want me to bring my cats to Cunningham, Anderson, Tate and Schwartz!" She practically screamed into the phone.

"It's true," Rita shouted.

"What are you talking about? Calm down," Norman said impatiently. "Where are you supposed to go?"

"To C.A.T. & S. The advertising agency making the commercial."

"Fantastic!" Norman said. "Elizabeth, start at the beginning. And speak slowly!"

Elizabeth took a deep breath. She gestured to Rita to be quiet. "C.A.T. & S. is the place I sent the pictures and application to and I just got their answer."

"What does it say?" Norman asked anxiously.

"I'll read it. 'Dear Ms. Dawson. An audition for your cats has been arranged for Thursday, May 17th at 11 o'clock for a Kitty Kat Cat Food television commercial. Please bring your cats to the 14th floor casting department at Cunningham, Anderson, Tate and Schwartz Advertising Agency, 550 Madison Avenue, New York City. Yours truly,' and it's signed by a Mr. Digby North. Doesn't that name sound important?"

"He's probably just some jerk in the casting department. Listen, this audition thing sounds good."

"Norman, I just know one of my cats will be chosen to be in the commercial with Clarence!"

"I hope you're right. After all, we're partners. But first things first. We've got to make arrangements for the audition. I guess you'd better tell your parents so that they can take you to the audition."

"No!"

"But you have to! How can they take you to the audition if you don't tell them? You can't walk!"

"They don't have to take me. I'm doing this on my own. Besides, you know my father works for

Purrfect Cat Food and he may not let me go."

"Lizzie, this is crazy. What if you get the job? Will he let you take it?"

"Getting a job is different from going to an audition."

"Lizzie, you're under age. If your father won't sign the contract, your cat can't do the commercial."

"Norman, I know that! Don't get so worried. If one of my cats gets the job, that will mean big money. There's a boy in my class who earned $8,000 in a toothpaste commercial! My parents would never turn it down. I'll just explain that no one at Dad's office has to know it's one of our cats. After all, they won't waste time in a commercial saying Snow Flake Dawson prefers Kitty Kat Food to Purrfect Cat Food."

"You never told me you were still going to keep this from your parents if you got the audition. You sure have a way of complicating things." Norman sounded irritated.

"Believe me, I can handle my parents. Why look for trouble before my cat gets the job? I wonder which cat they'll pick."

"Okay, Smarty, how are *you* going to get five cats from Edge Valley to New York City on the railroad during a school day?"

"Easy. You're going to help me!"

"Can I help too?" Rita whispered to Elizabeth.

"You're nuts!" Norman said.

"Please," Rita begged. Elizabeth ignored her.

"Where's your sense of adventure, Norman?

Do you want to spend the rest of your life down in the basement developing pictures and talking to a pet snake?"

"Cut it out!" Norman said angrily.

"Come on, Norman." She tried to sound coquettish. "Please help me this one last time." She paused. "Please!"

"Oh, maybe. But you're nuts . . . crazy . . . batty!"

"Come over here. My parents aren't home and we can make plans for May 17th."

Elizabeth hung up the phone.

"Can I go with you to the audition?" Rita pleaded.

"I don't think it's a good idea."

"Why not? I'm your best friend. And the letter came to *my* house."

"That has nothing to do with it. Norman is stronger. He can carry the cat carriers."

Rita frowned. "I helped you lug those carriers to school for Pet Day last year."

"Rita, this is different. It's a long trip and besides, if we are both out of school the same day, the Principal will know we're playing hookey."

Elizabeth didn't want to hurt her friend's feelings, but she really wanted to go alone with Norman. Quickly she added, "But I promise you'll come when the commerical is made. You'll spend the whole day at the studio."

"Promise?"

"Promise."

10

THURSDAY, MAY 17TH, WAS COOL AND overcast. The weatherman had predicted showers, but they hadn't started when Elizabeth arrived in the kitchen.

"First time I didn't have to call you for breakfast," Mrs. Dawson said.

"Dad left already?" Elizabeth asked.

Her mother nodded. "Elizabeth, about this pet show, is it really necessary to take all five cats?"

"Norman is helping me."

"I know, dear. But it looks like rain and it's such a bother to take three cat carriers!"

"Mom, we'll be fine on the bus."

"I'll be glad to drive you to school." Mrs. Dawson put a plate of scrambled eggs and toast in front of Elizabeth.

"No! I don't want you to drive me," she said quickly.

"Why not, dear? It's really no bother. I don't have any customers coming until after eleven."

Elizabeth stammered while eating the eggs. "I . . . I . . . the kids on the bus. I promised they could see the cats on the bus."

"Well, all right. But don't let those cats out of the boxes."

The back doorbell rang.

"That must be Norman." Elizabeth gulped down the apricot juice and ran from the table.

She opened the back door, and there was Norman, dressed for the city in a gray-green coat. He looked grimly at her.

"Some day for an adventure!" he grumbled.

Elizabeth put her finger to her mouth to indicate silence. "Mother's still here," she whispered.

He nodded. "Where are the cat boxes?"

"Upstairs in my bedroom. I've been up since five-thirty getting everything ready."

"Come in, Norman," Mrs. Dawson called. "Would you like a glass of milk or some apricot or carrot juice?"

"No, thank you, Mrs. Dawson," Norman said as he walked into the dinette area. "I've eaten. I've just come to help Lizzie with the cats."

"That's so nice of you, dear. Isn't her school bus out of your way?"

"Not really," Norman said. He flashed a quick frown toward Elizabeth. Elizabeth followed him out of the room.

"Don't forget to take your rain jacket, Elizabeth!"

They started up the stairs together. Norman whispered to her. "This is the dumbest thing I've ever gotten myself into. You are crazy." He was frowning again.

"Just think of it as fun!"

"Some fun if we get caught. It's called truancy, skipping school, playing hooky. There is a law against it."

She looked at him. He was certainly handsome, but he sure lacked that spark of adventure. There wasn't a drop of mischief in his eyes.

"Norman, leave it to me. Everything will go along as planned."

"I hope so."

"I cashed my birthday check from my grandparents," Elizabeth said, hoping to relieve Norman's anxiety. "It will pay for the train tickets."

Norman carried two carriers and Elizabeth one. They walked toward the bus stop and relaxed when they were out of sight of the Dawson house.

"Richie will be along about ten to nine. We can rest here." Norman said as they put the carriers down.

"That was a great idea asking your friend to give us a lift to the station. I didn't know you knew kids with licenses!" Elizabeth was very impressed.

"Junior license. He can only drive in the

county during daylight. I'll be able to take driver's ed a year from this fall," Norman said proudly.

"What's junior high like?" She was glad to be able to talk to him on a subject other than cats.

"It's a lot better than 6th grade. You get a different teacher every forty-five minutes."

"Thank goodness. Elementary is a real drag now. I'm sick of the same old faces."

"There's the car." Norman pointed to an old red Ford Pinto. The name "Fire Bird" was painted in black on the side.

Richie pulled over. Elizabeth recognized him from pictures in the local paper. He was the only sophomore allowed to play soccer on the varsity team! It was the hottest new sport in town and there had been a big write-up in the *Record*. She couldn't believe her good luck—meeting Richie Miller!

"Richie Miller, Lizzie, a . . . a . . . Elizabeth Dawson and cats!"

"Shove in," Richie said from behind the wheel.

Elizabeth smiled shyly and wiggled into the back seat behind the driver. The cat carriers went next to her.

Elizabeth let the boys do all the talking. She couldn't think of one clever remark to add to the front-seat conversation. In a few minutes they were deposited on the steps of the railroad station. It was almost empty now. The commuters had left an hour earlier.

Elizabeth took out her birthday money and

bought the two round-trip tickets. Then they managed to get themselves and the three cat carriers onto the platform. The New York train pulled in at exactly nine-eleven. They tried to ignore the incredulous stares of the other passengers. Norman insisted that they take the first car behind the engine because he hated smokers. They found two seats and settled down for the hour-and-fifteen-minute ride into the city.

Elizabeth was watching the backs of buildings that lined the tracks when she heard a familiar voice from behind her.

"Mother, I just can't stand that cigar smoke. I think I may throw up," the girl whined.

Elizabeth felt as though someone had hit her in the chest. Could it be? She was almost afraid to find out.

"This car will be better," a woman said.

"Mother! Look! I know that girl," the voice shrieked.

Elizabeth tried to shrink into her seat. There was no getting away from her.

Norman bent over and whispered, "Who is she?"

"Vivian," Elizabeth said with a mixture of hate and despair.

"Elizabeth Dawson, is that you?" Vivian said in her high nasal voice.

"No, Vivian," Elizabeth answered without turning around. "It isn't me. I just look like Elizabeth Dawson."

"Where are you going?"

Elizabeth didn't answer.

"*I* have an orthodontist's appointment. It's only for an evaluation."

"Vivian, go sit with your mother!" Elizabeth mumbled. "Or fall off the train."

"Well," she gave a sigh of exasperation. "I was only trying to be friendly. Norman Kelly and Elizabeth Dawson on a train to New York City. Does your mother know, Elizabeth?"

Norman turned around and stared at the thin, angular face. "Vivian, Elizabeth isn't in the mood to talk."

"Well! I bet you two are up to something and I'm going to find out what."

Elizabeth spun around. "You're a busybody and a troublemaker. Stay out of my life, Vivian. And if you tell my mother that you saw me on the train today you'll be sorry!"

Vivian gasped. Her eyes widened. "You wouldn't dare!" Vivian backed away from the seat.

"Try me!"

Vivian turned and ran to her seat next to her mother.

"That got her. Do you think she'll tell?" Elizabeth asked Norman. He was still grinning. He turned and looked at the mother and daughter team huddled in conversation in the back section of the car.

"I don't know if she'll tell *your* mother, but I'll bet you she's telling *her* mother right now."

"Rats! At least it's too late for my folks to stop us from going to the audition."

"And your parents will tell mine," Norman added grimly.

"Norman, it may be days before our mothers bump into each other. Stop worrying."

"Sure. Nothing to it. Just forget our cover story was blown"—Norman glanced at his watch—"fourteen minutes outside of town."

They rode in silence. Elizabeth watched suburban homes turn into shabby houses, then warehouses and factories. Finally the train went into a tunnel and everything was dark until the train lights went on.

"Only a few more minutes," Norman said. He pulled on his coat. Elizabeth did the same.

"Do you know where to get a taxi?" Elizabeth asked.

"We don't need one," he said. "The number four bus goes right up Madison Avenue. We're early anyway."

The train stopped. Elizabeth lifted one carrier and Norman took the other two. As they walked into the aisle to leave they saw Vivian and her mother in front of them. Both looked back at Elizabeth and Norman. Vivian pressed her lips tightly together and gave Elizabeth a mean, angry look.

11

THE BUILDING AT FIFTY-FOURTH
Street was new, tall, and modern. The front two
stories were all glass, and the doors opened automatically by electric eye. Inside everything was
marble. A starter dressed in a beige and choco-
late-brown uniform stood like a footman near the
elevators. He glared down at Elizabeth.

"You must want fourteen, Miss," he said for-
mally.

"Thank you," she said softly.

Norman followed Elizabeth into the first bank
of elevators. She pushed fourteen with her free
hand.

"You can put the carrier down," Norman commanded. "Nobody's going to steal it."

"Hold it!" a squeaky little voice shouted. Norman reached in front of Elizabeth and pushed the
hold button. A tiny old lady carrying a bundle in a

light-pink quilt rushed into the cubical. "Fourteen, please," she said breathlessly.

"Meow," said the bundle in her arms. Norman and Elizabeth looked at her in amazement.

"It's all right, sugar dear," the lady said. "Do you want to look?" she asked her two elevator companions. They nodded. Gently, the woman lowered the blanket. Inside was a white Persian cat with an elaborate rhinestone collar and a matching pink bow in her hair.

"Isn't she gorgeous?" the woman asked proudly. "She's won eighty-four blue ribbons. I see you have cats, too. What kinds do you specialize in?"

"Oh, every kind. I'm not particular. I'm more interested in brains than beauty," Elizabeth said.

"Well . . . I never." Just then, the elevator stopped at the fourteenth floor and the woman turned her back on them.

"You weren't very nice to her," Norman whispered as they picked up the carriers and stepped into the wide hall leading to the waiting room. "That cat is probably her whole life."

Elizabeth just shrugged.

Taped on the spotless bamboo wallpaper was a sign saying "Cat Casting, straight ahead." They followed the woman down the corridor and through a large glass door that said "Cunningham, Anderson, Tate and Schwartz Advertising Agency." Lining the walls were enlarged photographs of successful advertising campaigns.

Immediately, Elizabeth recognized the ad for "Sunshine," the soap powder, and "Bubbles," a new chocolate soda pop. Then a picture of Clarence licking his front paw next to a can of Kitty Kat Cat Food caught her attention. He was a handsome cat, she thought, but her cats were equally beautiful.

There were hordes of people in the waiting room with cats on leashes and cats in carriers. Only about ten people were lucky enough to be seated on couches. Others were either sitting on the floor with their feline companions or leaning against a wall.

In the center of the room was a large metal desk. A beautifully groomed young woman was sitting majestically behind it. "Mr. Ralph Smith and Fifi," she called loudly.

A man sitting on the far wall jumped up.

"Come, Fifi," he called. A long-haired black cat with her tail held high followed him across the room.

"You can go into that office now," said the receptionist pointing to another glass door. The man's seat was instantly filled by a young woman holding a cat in a wicker basket. The cat was busy licking a little green lollipop that the woman held out to her.

A woman carrying a calico cat exited into the waiting room. "You were very naughty," she said loudly to her pet.

The little old lady was talking to the receptionist. Elizabeth watched as she was told to wait and find a place to sit.

Elizabeth stepped up to the desk. "Your name?"

"Elizabeth Dawson. I brought five cats."

"Five! Dawson . . . Dawson, yes. You're early. I'm afraid all these people and cats are ahead of you."

"That's okay."

The lady wrote her name on a paper attached to a clipboard and put a check next to the one listing appointment times.

"Here," Norman called from an empty floor space near a large potted plant. She carried her case over to him and they both sat cross-legged on the floor.

"I'm nervous," Elizabeth whispered to Norman. "We're the only kids here." They both looked around the room. The reception area was dominated by older, well-dressed women. Each was chattering to the other strangers nearby and petting a cat. A few men used carriers, but most of the animals were content to be on their owners' laps or at their feet.

"Maybe you should let your cats out so they can get some air," Norman suggested.

"Are you nuts?" she cried. "I'll never get them back into the boxes."

"Look at these cats, Lizzie. They don't look real." Norman looked around the room and shook his head.

"I know what you mean," Elizabeth felt uncomfortable. "I don't have a chance. These cats are really trained."

A well-dressed lady bent over and interrupted them. She smiled and said, "It's so nice to see young people in the business. Tell me, how many cats did you bring?"

"Five," Norman answered.

"My goodness, five talented cats. I only have Josephine here." She patted the thin beige cat on her lap. "She's very musical. If I hum the Mexican Hat Dance, she'll meow when you're supposed to clap."

"Terrific," Elizabeth said sarcastically. Norman gave her one of his "cool it" looks.

Just then the man in the trench coat next to her chimed in, "My darling can shake either paw." With that, he extended his right hand, and the striped cat immediately held up hers. "What do your cats do?"

Elizabeth hesitated. "They act like cats!"

"But do they do any special tricks?" asked the heavy-set woman standing near the artificial tree. "My Lulu can fix her own dinner."

"By catching a mouse," Norman whispered to Elizabeth. She cracked up.

The man on the couch took a bagel out of his pocket. "Watch this," he commanded of the little audience in Elizabeth's section of the reception area. With a toss of his hand, he threw the bagel into the air, and the cat sprang up and caught it in her paw like in a loop toss game. The two women applauded.

"Norman," Elizabeth said, turning her back to the gentleman and speaking softly, "I think we're in trouble. My cats can't do anything. In fact, I don't even know if I'll be able to get them back into the carriers after I let them out!"

"Play it cool, Lizzie. After all, C.A.T. & S. didn't advertise for a bagel-catching, singing cat that can shake hands!"

"No, but they *did* ask for *trained* cats. I wish I'd never come."

"That's not like you, partner. We're here, so let's give it all we've got. After all, we have nothing to lose."

"Except my cats!" Elizabeth moaned.

One by one, each cat owner was called by the receptionist and disappeared through the glass door behind her desk.

"The man with the bagel cat was inside a long time," Elizabeth commented.

"Good sign," the chubby lady said. She petted Lulu rapidly. "If they like you, they video tape. Otherwise, it's out, one, two, three."

"How do you know?" asked Norman.

"Oh, Lulu has been to other auditions. And she was an extra in two movies."

"What did Lulu do as an extra?" Elizabeth asked.

"She didn't have a real role like in this Kitty Kat commercial," the lady said. "Lulu just walked across a street in one film and sat under a tree in the other. She was paid for a day's work!"

"For being a cat?" Norman asked.

The lady nodded. "Now this job is big, *real* big. There will be thousands of dollars in residuals."

"What are residuals?" Norman asked.

"You really are new in the business. Residuals are payments the actor or in this case the cat gets every time the commercial is shown on TV."

"Wow! or should I say MEOW!" Norman said.

"There have been cat calls out all over the city," the chubby lady said, "Who's your agent?"

"We don't have one. I just sent in some pictures and they wrote to me."

"I hate to say this, but you really don't have much of a chance. This is a very closed business. You *must* have an agent. Mr. North will never take you seriously."

Elizabeth frowned. "Well, we'll see."

"Mrs. Katz and Lulu," the receptionist called. The woman rose and smiled at Elizabeth.

"Good luck, dear."

Elizabeth didn't feel like returning the remark or the smile, but she did anyway.

Norman looked at his watch. "Let's see how long Mrs. Know-it-all is in her audition." It was twenty minutes after eleven. Elizabeth realized that they had been sitting at C.A.T. & S. for one hour, and their scheduled appointment time had passed.

"Maybe we'll never be called," she said to Norman.

He continued to stare at his watch. "Everyone that's been called was here before us. Our turn will come."

"Oops! There she is!" Elizabeth waved to Mrs. Katz. Norman looked up from his watch.

"Four minutes," he said to Elizabeth. "They couldn't have video taped Lulu."

"She's avoiding us," Elizabeth said. Mrs. Katz walked quickly out the door mumbling to herself.

"Dawson . . . Miss Elizabeth Dawson and cats!" The receptionist's voice sent a shock through Elizabeth's body.

"That's me!" she cried out loudly. Everyone in the room turned and looked at her.

"Use the door behind me," the receptionist said.

"The cats!" Elizabeth shrieked.

"I've got two boxes," Norman called. He fumbled and almost fell into the plant. "You get that one," he ordered as he regained his balance.

Together they walked through the door and into a long white hall. The door closed automatically behind them. A thin woman's voice came from behind another door. Elizabeth felt trapped.

"Mrs. Dawson, come in with your cat."

"Can I bring my friend with me? I can't carry all the carriers," Elizabeth said timidly in the direction of the voice.

There was silence. Suddenly a tall, slender young woman appeared at the doorway. She had an expression of surprise on her face the moment she saw the young pair. "Why, you're a girl!"

"Yes, Miss . . . a . . . a . . . and he's a boy . . . I mean he's my business partner, Norman Kelly."

The woman smiled. "Miss Dawson and Mr. Kelly, please come in. Mr. North expected a somewhat older couple. Your cat glossies were very professionally done."

"Thank you," Norman said shyly.

"Let me help you with a carrier." She took one box from Norman and led them into a room the size of the Dawson's living room. There was a conference table at the far end near a full-length window. One man, rather plump and with a gray receding hairline, was sitting, shuffling through papers and pictures on the table. Elizabeth hoped he would be as friendly as the woman.

"Mr. North, we have the next applicant. Miss Dawson and her cats—five."

The man looked up. He smiled automatically. "Five cats?" he asked.

Elizabeth nodded. She noted a tone of surprise in Mr. North's voice.

"Okay, honey, let's see them do their tricks."

Elizabeth cleared her voice, then took a deep breath. "Mr. North, my cats don't do *tricks*. They are not circus entertainers. They are cat cats and they eat Kitty Kat Cat Food."

"Which case do you want me to open first?" Norman whispered.

"Go on, Miss . . . Miss Dawson. We're looking for real cats. Let's see them." Mr. North leaned back in his chair. His face was expressionless.

The assistant closed the door.

"Okay, Norman, open them up. I'll do the talking."

Norman unsnapped each carrier. Tinker Bell was the first to lift up her little gray striped head above the top of the carrier. Quickly she jumped out of the box and raced around the office. Elizabeth ignored her and continued to talk directly to Mr. North.

"I've been raised with cats all my life. In fact, each year for my birthday I've been given another kitten. Did you know that more money is spent on pet food than on baby food in America? And cats know one cat food from another. You can't feed any old thing to your cat. I know, because I've tried. My cats prefer Kitty Kat. All my cats prefer Kitty Kat."

Snow Flake walked right across the conference table and jumped under it. Cat was rubbing against Elizabeth's legs. As Elizabeth talked she scratched her. Mr. North motioned to his assistant to cross the room to the camera facing the wall.

As soon as the assistant's chair was vacant, Princess Margaret jumped out of the carrier and leaped onto the chair. She curled into a tight ball and ignored everything around her. She even yawned.

"Every cat has her own personality," Elizabeth continued. "That's Princess Margaret. She's a loner and very sophisticated. If she ate at a restaurant she'd order filet mignon, but she loves Kitty Kat."

Elizabeth looked for a smile on Mr. North's face but there was none. How was she doing? He gave her no clue.

"Continue," he said. Then he shouted orders to his assistant. "Did you get that?"

The assistant was behind the camera. A little red light was on and she was guiding the machine with a long handle.

"Please go on, Miss Dawson." He looked down at his sheet. "Elizabeth, continue! Tell me about your cats."

Mr. North still did not show any emotion, just extreme politeness. But he was taping! Elizabeth was determined to please him. "I . . . I . . . " she started to stutter as she looked at the camera.

"Forget about the camera. Don't even bother facing it. Tell me about the calico cat now."

Ezmeralda jumped onto the conference table. "Ezmeralda is the most curious of all my cats. She loves boxes and papers." Elizabeth hesitated as Ezmeralda headed for a pile of photographs on the table. "There she goes right to your papers! You see, she's a curious calico, but when it comes to cat food she wants her favorite brand. She's not the least bit curious about other brands. Shall I get her, Mr. North?"

"Maybe you'd better put her back in her box, Elizabeth. But first hold her in your arms so that we can get a shot."

Elizabeth did as she was told, then handed Ezmeralda to Norman who dropped in and snapped the box closed. She looked at Mr. North. He was smiling broadly now or was he laughing. She couldn't tell.

"Elizabeth, hold up each cat in turn so we can get them on tape," Mr. North directed.

"Okay, I'll try, Mr. North."

"And get a shot of Princess Margaret on the chair. See if you can catch her yawning," he told the assistant. "Keep on talking, Elizabeth," he ordered firmly. He was serious again.

"About what?"

"You certainly seem to know a lot about cats and cat food, so why don't you just tell us some more?"

Mr. North leaned back in his chair. Elizabeth felt he was judging her. It was now that she would make it or lose it.

Elizabeth lifted up Cat. She was smooth and slippery and didn't want to stay in her arms.

"Cat loves to eat salad. Not lettuce and tomatoes with dressing, but grass and the bushes around our house. It's very good for cats. I mean, eating a good nutritious cat food like Kitty Kat plus some green. It helps improve their digestion." Cat jumped down and into the wastepaper basket. "Get her, Norman," Elizabeth yelled.

Cat pushed the basket over and scrambled out, scattering the contents on the floor. Norman started chasing Cat around the room. Tinker Bell thought it was a new game and joined the chase. The assistant tried to corner them but missed. Snow Flake watched from the window sill and licked her paw, while Princess Margaret stayed on the chair, pulling herself into a tighter ball and yawning.

"Stay by the camera!" Mr. North ordered.

"I just thought I'd help," the assistant cried as she grabbed the handle again and the red light flickered on.

"They're just teasing, Mr. North. If we ignore Tinker Bell and Cat, they'll stop." She walked over to the window and picked up Snow Flake. She allowed herself to be petted and lifted into Elizabeth's arms.

"Snow Flake is conceited. She thinks she's the most beautiful cat in the world and she loves attention. She'd be the perfect model for a Rolls Royce car. And do you know what? She eats Kitty Kat Cat Food too! Norman, please put her in the carrier and just ignore Cat and Tinker Bell."

When he took the little white cat out of her arms, Norman whispered, "You're terrific. Keep it up."

"I hope I can con the others into the carrier," she whispered back.

Elizabeth had no trouble with Princess Margaret, but Tinker Bell and Cat just would not stop chasing each other around the room. They slipped and slid on the shiny white tile floor. Finally Mr. North had an idea. He went into the back room and came out with a plate and an open can of Kitty Kat.

"Keep the camera rolling," he said as he emptied the food onto the paper plate. He put the plate down near the two playful cats.

Elizabeth and Norman stood still. Elizabeth crossed her fingers and said a silent prayer, "Let them eat it, please!"

The cats didn't stop to notice the food. They continued to circle. Elizabeth felt shattered. Then Norman went to the plate and gently shook it. "Here Tinker Bell! Here Cat!" he called softly, but with a tint of command in his voice.

Suddenly, the cats stopped running. First Tinker Bell looked at Norman and the food. She walked to it carefully. She lowered her head and inspected the contents. No one said a word. They both began to eat.

"Get a close-up!" Mr. North whispered to his assistant.

Elizabeth and Norman looked at each other and smiled.

"Elizabeth, do you have any control over your cats?" Mr. North asked as he watched the two cats eat.

"Well, yes and no," she hedged. "What I mean is that I *know* what *they'll* do, but I can't *tell* them what to do. They're very independent cats."

"And those two," he said, pointing in the direction of the two eating. "Are they always so wild?"

Elizabeth didn't know what to say. She was trapped. "Tinker Bell is very playful. If Cat hadn't started acting silly, she wouldn't have taken off around the room. Really, Mr. North, it only happens when the two of them are together, but they *love* Kitty Kat Food!"

"Yes, I can see that," he said and smiled.

Elizabeth felt relieved.

"Princess Margaret and Snow Flake are exceptionally beautiful and well-behaved," he said.

"They like Kitty Kat Food too!" Elizabeth added quickly.

"I'm sure they do."

Norman and Elizabeth picked up Cat and Tinker Bell the moment the plate was empty. Norman put them into their carriers.

Mr. North pushed a button on his telephone and said, "Please have Mr. Cunningham and Mr. Schwartz step into my office before lunch." Then he looked at Elizabeth and Norman and said in a cool, businesslike way, "Thank you for coming. We'll call you."

Elizabeth picked up one carrier. She wondered if he meant he really would call or did he mean, "Don't call us, we'll call you"?

As soon as all the cat carriers were filled, Norman and Elizabeth went back to the waiting room. The crowd had thinned. Norman put down one of the carriers and looked at his watch.

"Wow! Elizabeth, you'll never believe this!"

"What?" She was deep in her own thoughts. Did Mr. North like her cats?

"We were in there twenty-seven minutes!"

"You're kidding!" She looked at his wrist-watch.

"Nope. I just timed it! Maybe, just maybe, one of your cats will be picked!"

"Norman, this is like one big crazy dream. Twenty-seven minutes, and we *were* video taped, too!"

"Well, partner, we may be in business!"

12

THEY MADE THE TWO-FOURTEEN train back to Edge Valley. Luckily no one they knew was on it. Elizabeth didn't even try to make conversation with Norman. She was too busy daydreaming about the future and reliving the morning's audition. They took the local bus to her house. There were a few familiar faces on it, but no one seemed to stare at them peculiarly. Besides, school was over so they weren't the only kids on the bus.

They reached their stop and Norman walked Elizabeth to her back door. He put down the two carriers and said, "If you hear anything, I don't care if it's in the middle of the night, call me!"

"Sure. Don't worry. It's not going to happen overnight. They have to have conferences and things."

"Lizzie, I just want to tell you again, I thought you did a fantastic job. Talking the way you did about Kitty Kat Cat Food. It was some sales pitch."

Elizabeth blushed. "You did a swell job, too. I never could have gotten into the city alone."

"Thanks. Now don't forget to keep in touch," he said as he walked down the back steps. He gave her a final wave and smiled as he turned the corner around the house.

Elizabeth held the screen door open with her back while she managed to open the door. One by one she lifted the carriers into the house.

"Is that you, Elizabeth?" Her mother's voice filled the house.

"Yes, Mom." She bent down and opened the tops of the carriers. The cats hopped out. Immediately they went to their favorite spots in the kitchen after stopping at the water dish. They held their tails up high indicating to Elizabeth that they were happy to be home and out of show business.

"Come into the living room *now!*" the voice demanded.

"Coming," Elizabeth said meekly. Something in her mother's tone of voice made Elizabeth's heart drop to her stomach. Had Vivian told so soon?

She walked through the kitchen into the hall and stepped into the living room.

She couldn't believe her eyes! "Daddy! What

are you doing home?" Her heart sank to her toes. There must have been a major tragedy, she thought. Maybe someone died! Her father never came home early except for something serious.

"Why do you think I'm home?" he asked sternly.

Her brain screamed: They know! They know! I'm dead! She flopped into a chair and stared down at the floor.

"Shall we just say the cat's out of the bag?" her mother said. Her face was strained. "I received a very friendly call this afternoon from Vivian's mother. She casually asked where you were going on the train this morning with three big cat carriers and Norman Kelly."

Elizabeth mumbled under her breath. "I'll get her."

"I didn't have the slightest idea what she was talking about, so I said she must have been mistaken. I must have sounded like a total fool. She was positive it was you! After she hung up I called the school and you were reported absent! Then I called your father."

An invisible rope was closing around Elizabeth's neck. She could hardly swallow.

"Elizabeth," her father said in his deepest, most serious voice, "where were you and what are you up to? I want an explanation, and I want it now!"

Elizabeth sank further into her chair. She wished she could make herself invisible, the way she had seen it done in a movie. Should she tell her father the truth? Her mouth quivered as she began to speak. "I . . . we took the cats, just the female ones, to New York City to have some pictures taken."

"What kind of pictures?" her father demanded.

Elizabeth hesitated. A little white lie wouldn't hurt and, besides, nothing might ever come of the audition anyway.

After a long moment of silence, Elizabeth said, "It was a sort of contest. These people I went to see wanted to find the prettiest and most talented cats in the city. That's all there was to it."

Mr. Dawson looked skeptical. "What did they want the pictures for?"

Elizabeth shrugged and tried to sound very casual. "Oh, I don't know exactly. Maybe for a magazine or some kind of publicity."

Elizabeth knew she was being too evasive. She sensed that her father knew he was on to something.

"Who are 'these people' you went to see?" Mr. Dawson asked.

Elizabeth felt cornered. There was no way to retreat. She said very softly, as though to minimize the impact of her statement, "Cunningham, Anderson, Tate and Schwartz."

Mr. Dawson looked at Elizabeth with disbelieving eyes. "You what!" he exploded. "An advertising agency! They handle the Kitty Kat account. There can be only one reason why they want your cats. For a commercial!"

Elizabeth nodded and tears began to form in her eyes and blur her vision. She tried to explain. Her voice was weak and apologetic. "I saw an ad for auditions for a female cat to play in a commercial with Clarence. I wrote to the advertising agency telling them about my five female cats."

"But you know I work for Purrfect Cat Food Company," Mr. Dawson said angrily. "Kitty Kat is our biggest competitor. Did you ever think of that?"

Elizabeth made no reply.

"You did it behind our backs!" Mrs. Dawson said reproachfully. "You shouldn't have done that."

"I didn't want to upset you," Elizabeth said.

"Well, you've certainly managed to upset us now," her father shouted. He waved his arms around the room. "Where do you think all this came from? From Purrfect Cat Food, that's where! I've worked like a dog to make Purrfect Cat Food the *best* cat food."

Elizabeth smiled a little smile. "That's funny, Daddy," she said, trying to break the tension. "Working like a dog for cat food."

Her father did not return the smile. "There's nothing funny about it. You're a traitor, that's what you are. Imagine! My very own daughter runs off and sells out on me. She goes off and makes a commercial for Kitty Kat Cat Food, my biggest rival. It's like being stabbed in the back!"

"But I didn't make a commercial. I only went to an audition."

"I'm sure Elizabeth didn't mean any harm," Mrs. Dawson said.

For a moment Mr. Dawson seemed to calm down. "Why didn't you tell me?" he asked.

"I don't know. I'm sorry."

"You didn't tell me because you knew I wouldn't let you go. Isn't that the reason?"

Elizabeth nodded. "I thought if I got the job, it would mean a lot of money and maybe you'd let me do it. I mean, let the cats do it."

"Never! I won't let those darn cats work for a competitive cat food company."

"They'd be scratching the hands that feed them," Mrs. Dawson added.

"But no one has to ever know they're *our* cats," Elizabeth protested.

"I don't care. I won't allow it!" Mr. Dawson said with finality.

Elizabeth couldn't hold back her tears. They began to run down her face.

Mrs. Dawson tried to calm her husband. "They may not even pick one of our cats for the commercial. So all this arguing is pointless."

"That's right," Elizabeth said eagerly. "There were some gorgeous cats at the audition." Then she added with pride, "But my cats were wonderful too."

"We'll wait and see," her father said. "But

remember this, if that agency contacts you again, you're to tell me immediately."

Elizabeth nodded.

"You still deserve a punishment," Mrs. Dawson said. "You did all this behind our backs."

"I'm sorry, Mom," Elizabeth said. "I really am. I just got deeper and deeper into it. I'll polish your silver for the rest of my life, if you want me to."

"You'll help me if I need help," Mrs. Dawson said, "but that's not enough. To start with, since you're so hooked on TV commercials, let's see if we can unhook you. Television is off limits until you've learned how to stay out of mischief. At the rate you've been going that could be years!"

Mr. Dawson leaned back in his chair and concentrated. "I feel you have too much time on your hands, Elizabeth. You're too young for a paying job, but I'm going to see about getting you something to do at the Purrfect Company Cat Kennel on a volunteer basis." He was still frowning.

"I'd like that," she said. She tried to smile, but she couldn't.

"I feel you need more structure in your life. Perhaps being an only child has made your imagination go wild. Now go to your room."

She stood up. The tears were still flowing and she couldn't look at her parents. "I'm sorry. I really am," she said and ran out of the room.

13

THE NEXT MORNING NORMAN WAS waiting outside Elizabeth's house.

"Hi!" he said weakly. "Did I get it from my parents!" Elizabeth noticed that his eyes had gray pockets under them, and his shirt was wrinkled. She suspected that he had slept in it.

"Me, too," Elizabeth said. Even the idea of Norman walking her to the school bus stop didn't cheer her up.

"The snake is going back to Pete's Pet Shop. I was really getting very fond of the little fellow."

"Is that your only punishment?"

"Are you kidding? I was going to get special developing equipment for my birthday, but it's been nixed. This is the pits!"

"I'm sorry, Norman. I really got you into a mess."

"You sure did. But to tell the truth, it was a lot of fun." He flashed a quick grin. "Listen, what are you going to do if the advertising agency calls?"

"My father said no . . . absolutely no. I can't work for a rival cat food company no matter how much they offer."

"I was afraid of that." They were now at the corner. Rita started running toward them.

"Hey, Elizabeth, wait for me!" she shouted. She was breathless when she reached them.

"Hi, Rita," Elizabeth said casually. She noticed that Rita smiled at Norman and gave her an approving nod. She knew it would be all over the 6th grade that Norman Kelly had walked Elizabeth Dawson to the bus stop. Not bad, she thought, even if it's for the wrong reason.

"Am I glad I didn't go with you yesterday. Vivian is a skunk. She's telling everybody she saw you playing hooky."

"Big mouth. I hope I can return the favor someday."

"Here comes your bus," Norman said. "When this thing blows over, I'd like to take your picture alone, without the cats. Okay?"

"Sure. Great." She felt a spurt of happiness but it faded quickly when she remembered this wasn't going to just "blow over." Elizabeth joined the people on line at the stop and waved to Norman as she stepped onto the bus.

School was terrific for a change. Elizabeth was

the center of attention. She told her friends about the trip to New York and the audition.

"Why do they video tape?" a friend asked.

"So they can play it back later in front of the producer and director. Mr. North is the head of casting, but he doesn't make the final decision." She answered all their questions and felt very important.

After school, Elizabeth did her homework and stayed in her room. At four o'clock the telephone rang. Her mother was in the basement selling antiques so Elizabeth answered it. "Hello," she said into the phone.

"Is this Miss Dawson, Miss Elizabeth Dawson?" a female voice asked. Elizabeth instantly recognized it. It was Mr. North's assistant.

"It's me. I'm Elizabeth Dawson." She started to shake. Was this really happening? Was C.A.T. & S. really calling her?

"This is the casting office of Cunningham, Anderson, Tate and Schwartz. We would like you to bring a cat named Princess Margaret into New York again for a personal interview with Mr. Horace Cunningham and Mr. Benjamin Schwartz."

"Oh no! I can't," whimpered Elizabeth. She was in a total state of shock.

"We'd like you to bring a parent or guardian with you for this meeting since you are under age."

"I can't," she repeated, only louder this time.

"Is tomorrow inconvenient? We can make the appointment for another day," said the assistant.

"No. You don't understand. I can't come at all."

"Perhaps you'd better speak to Mr. North." The phone was dead. Elizabeth could hear whispers in the background. Finally Mr. North came on the line.

"Elizabeth, what's the problem?" Mr. North asked. He sounded very friendly.

"It's my father," she said and paused. Should she tell him the whole truth? "He doesn't want my cats to be in a Kitty Kat commercial."

"Didn't you tell him you were auditioning them?" he asked. There was a tone of surprise in his voice.

"No. I should have, but I didn't," Elizabeth admitted.

"Well, perhaps if I spoke to him. We're very interested in Princess Margaret."

"My father isn't here. He's working."

"Let me see. You live in Edge Valley, right?" he asked.

"Yes. Why?"

"I live only two towns away in the Cove. Why don't I drive over tonight and speak to your father myself?"

Elizabeth didn't know what to say. She started to stutter. "I . . . I don't know. I'll have to ask my mother. Hold on a minute. She's in the basement." Elizabeth ran to the foot of the stairs and yelled. At first there was no answer. She called again. Her mother answered with her usual "Yes?"

"Are you and Daddy going to be home tonight?"

"Yes. We have no plans. Why?"

"Mr. North wants to drive over and speak to you."

"That will be fine. I have some lovely pieces of silver to show him."

Elizabeth realized that her mother thought she had said Mr. Norton. He was a regular customer. Well, she could pretend she hadn't heard. Her heart began to pound with excitement.

"Hello, Mr. North. My parents will be home tonight."

"Good. I'll drive over after dinner, about eight. You live at 16 Avon Road."

"Oh wait! My address is 25 Mountainview Lane. It's just around the corner from Avon Road."

"But that's not the same as on your application."

"I know. Er . . . well . . . I used someone else's address, Rita Shaw's, because . . . because she's my assistant." Elizabeth fumbled.

"All right. I'll see you at eight o'clock at 25 Mountainview Lane. Goodbye."

"Goodbye, Mr. North," she said and hung up. Her heart was still pounding with a steady beat. She picked up the phone again, and dialed. It rang and rang and rang. Finally someone answered.

"Norman!"

"Yes. I was in the dark room, Lizzie. What's up?"

"The agency called."

"No! Wild!"

"Mr. North is coming over tonight to our house to talk to my parents about using Princess Margaret."

"You're kidding!"

"Nope. How about coming over?"

"I don't think I'm welcome." The enthusiasm dropped from his voice.

"Just use an excuse. Say something like you have some more pictures for me. And act surprised when you see Mr. North," she ordered.

"Are you sure your mother isn't going to throw me out?"

"Norman, where's your nerve? Just come over by eight and don't worry so much."

"Okay. To tell you the truth, this is one scene I wouldn't want to miss for a million dollars. What are the chances of changing your father's mind?"

"Who knows? But I'm going to give it one more big try. See you at eight."

14

At seven-thirty, Elizabeth walked into the television room and approached her father during a commercial break.

"Mr. North is coming over at eight o'clock to talk to you," she said as casually as she could.

He continued to watch the screen. "No, dear, Mr. Norton is coming to look at some silver for his shop."

"No, Dad. Maybe Mom misunderstood. Mr. North from C.A.T. & S. is coming over tonight to talk to you about Princess Margaret." Her father turned away from the tube and glared at her.

"What are you up to now!" he demanded.

"Nothing. It was *his* idea. He only lives in the Cove. He wants to talk to you. He called me. I didn't call him."

"There is nothing to talk about. Princess Margaret cannot appear in a Kitty Kat commercial. Call him back and tell him not to bother coming."

"I don't know his telephone number."

"Look in the book!" He was fuming now.

The doorbell rang.

"Maybe that's him." Elizabeth said. Her father ignored her completely. She left him staring at the screen and mumbling under his breath. She ran down the stairs and opened the door.

Norman faced her. "I'm a little early." He was carrying a package. "I brought some more proofs for you to see. Maybe you'd like to give them to your parents as a peace offering." He seemed unusually shy.

"Gee, am I glad you're here! I'm afraid my father isn't going to come out of the TV room when Mr. North comes. He's really burning."

"Oh, I bet he will. He won't be rude. How did you manage to set up this meeting?"

"It wasn't *my* idea. It was Mr. North's. Come into the living room and we'll wait." He followed her. "Even if my father won't come down, I know my mother will at least be polite." Elizabeth was beginning to get a little nervous. "Let's see the proofs."

He pulled them out of the envelope. "I took these while you were trying to get the cats back into the carriers. I think they're really fun shots."

Elizabeth laughed at the crazy expressions on her face. They were chattering away when the doorbell rang again.

"That must be *him!*" Elizabeth shouted. She looked at Norman. "I think I'm going to die."

"Before you do that, answer the door," Norman said, trying to sound calm, but his face turned pale. "We have nothing to lose now."

It rang again. Elizabeth took a deep breath, pulled down her polo shirt, and walked into the hall. Norman followed. They faced the door. Slowly she turned the knob. Inch by inch she opened the door.

Mr. North was standing in front of her. He smiled immediately and extended his arm. "Well, Elizabeth, hello." He shook her hand. "And Mr. Kelly, the photographer." He shook Norman's hand too.

Norman beamed shyly.

"Won't you come in," Elizabeth said. "I'll get my parents. Norman will show you to the living room."

"Thank you." He followed Norman.

Elizabeth stopped for a moment in the hallway to take a few quick breaths. Madame Rollin had recommended it for stage fright. She went into the kitchen. Her mother was making a grocery list.

"Mr. North is here."

She looked up. "You mean, Mr. Norton." She put down her pencil and started across the kitchen.

"No. Mr. Digby North. He's from Cunningham, Anderson, Tate and Schwartz."

Mrs. Dawson stopped in the middle of the room. "What?" she almost screamed.

Elizabeth put her finger to her lips. "He'll hear you!"

"What is someone from that agency doing here?"

"I told you this afternoon. He called and asked if he could talk to you and Daddy tonight. You said you'd be home."

"But I thought you said Mr. Norton, Jim Norton."

"Mom, he's here in the living room. Please talk to him. I told him you won't let me use Princess Margaret in a Kitty Kat commercial."

"All right. Call your father."

"Maybe *you'd* better. He's mad at me."

In a few minutes Mr. and Mrs. Dawson were both shaking hands with Mr. North while Norman and Elizabeth watched.

"I'm sorry you took this trip for nothing," Mr. Dawson said. "My cats cannot be in a Kitty Kat Cat Food commercial."

"Why are you so against it, Mr. Dawson?" Mr. North asked politely as he settled into the couch and crossed his legs. He just couldn't seem to believe that Mr. Dawson would object. "We don't harm our animals in any way and it pays very well."

"Oh, I'm sure you don't harm the cats you work with. That's not the point."

Mr. North looked confused. "If it's money

you're concerned about, Princess Margaret will get full residuals."

"There are more important things than money," Mr. Dawson said rather pompously.

Mr. North looked bewildered. He shook his head from side to side. "I don't understand. When we send out a call for animals to be used in our commercials the reception room is filled with people eager to get their pets on TV. Now, we're eager to use Princess Margaret, and for some unknown reason, you don't want to go along with the idea. I don't understand, Mr. Dawson."

"There's a very good reason for my decision," Mr. Dawson said. "I appreciate your interest in Princess Margaret, and realize you went out of your way to come here, but I still can't let you use her."

The look of bewilderment never left Mr. North's face. "But *why?*" he asked. "Just give me one good reason."

Mr. Dawson took a deep breath. He glanced at Elizabeth. She looked bitterly disappointed. Her moment of triumph had turned to defeat. At that moment, almost on cue, Princess Margaret walked into the room. She walked proudly and with dignity, like the princess she was. She leaped gracefully onto the couch and looked at Mr. Dawson, and it seemed to Elizabeth that there was a pleading look in her eyes.

"Well," Mr. North said, "what is your reason?" His eyes challenged Mr. Dawson.

"You see, I work for the Purrfect Cat Food Company. I've worked for them for years. I'm an executive with the company. As you well know, Kitty Kat is our biggest competitor. I can't have our cat make a commercial for a rival company. It's a matter of integrity! I am loyal to my company and so are my cats."

Then Mr. North did a most unexpected thing. He leaned back and his lips began to curl upward. His smile broke into a laugh that became so boisterous, he couldn't stop laughing. Princess Margaret stood up on the couch and, with one continuous leap, pounced right into Mr. North's arms. He held her close. "Don't worry, Princess," he said, stroking the cat fondly. "You'll still be on TV."

"I don't understand," Mr. Dawson said. "Didn't you hear what I said?"

"I heard you," Mr. North replied. "Now I know why your daughter knew so much about cats and cat food. She was magnificent. She could have a copywriter's job any day at C.A.T. & S."

"What has that got to do with Princess Margaret going on a Kitty Kat commercial? My decision still stands."

"Calm down," Mr. North said. "Just take it easy. I never said we wanted Princess Margaret for the Kitty Kat account."

"What do you mean?" Mr. Dawson asked.

"I don't understand," Elizabeth interrupted. "I auditioned for Kitty Kat."

"Let me explain. There's a new decaffeinated coffee coming out and we've got the account. We've been looking for a new angle for the commercial for months and, when I ran your video tape for Mr. Cunningham and Mr. Schwartz, we all agreed—Princess Margaret is our new angle!"

"But Princess Margaret doesn't drink coffee," Elizabeth said. Then she added eagerly, "But maybe if she tried it, she'd like it."

Once again Mr. North laughed uproariously. "That won't be necessary," he said. "Listen to this: 'You'll sleep like a kitten with Royal decaffeinated coffee.' I know Princess Margaret isn't exactly a kitten, but when we photograph her in a large chair, she'll look like one and she won't grow out of the part. Now, how's that for an advertising campaign?"

"I don't believe it!" Elizabeth whispered to Norman.

"Unreal!" Norman said a little shyly.

"What about the Kitty Kat commercial?" Elizabeth asked.

"Let me explain," Mr. North answered. "In the tape all your cats were running wild. You remember that, don't you Elizabeth?"

"I remember. Controlling them was a problem."

"They're untrained. We could never use them in a commercial with Clarence. But during all that commotion, Princess Margaret behaved royally. She sat calmly in the chair with a sophisticated

air, as you yourself described her. She's exactly what we're looking for to sell this new decaffeinated coffee.

"I just can't believe it!" Elizabeth blurted out. "It's too good to be true."

"Fantastic!" Norman chimed in.

Elizabeth turned to her father. "Now, can they use Princess Margaret, Dad? Please!"

Mr. Dawson cleared his throat. He smiled, and this time it was his turn to laugh. "Well, since it's not for a competitive product, I don't see why not."

"Hurray!" Elizabeth screamed. She jumped up and threw her arms around her father. "Oh, thank you, Daddy! Oh, thank you!"

"Thank Mr. North," Mr. Dawson said. "He saved the day."

Mr. North put Princess Margaret down, opened his briefcase and took out a sheaf of papers. "I brought the contract with me, and I think this is as good a time as ever to celebrate by signing it."

"Oh, I'm so happy," Elizabeth cried.

"It's a standard contract," Mr. North said. "But if you want to go over it with your lawyer, we could put off the signing."

"That probably won't be necessary," Mr. Dawson said.

As Princess Margaret's legal guardian, Mr. Dawson read and signed the contract. Just as he was about to hand it back to Mr. North, Princess Margaret began to meow.

"I guess she wants to sign also," Mr. North said and smiled. He picked Princess Margaret up again and very gently took her paw and pressed it to the bottom of the contract. "Now everything is quite legal," he said.

Just then cats started to appear from everywhere. Tinker Bell came from under the couch, while Cat and Ezmeralda leaped from behind a chair. Snow Flake jumped off of the window sill and led the parade into the center of the room.

"They don't want to miss the celebration," Elizabeth said.

A slinky red-haired tomcat leaped to the top of the piano, hitting a few notes along the way. A lovely Siamese cat with soft blue eyes crept into Mrs. Dawson's lap, while a huge black cat with white paws curled up next to Mr. Dawson purring happily. Then Softie, the little beige kitten, came tumbling in and Elizabeth picked her up and petted her tenderly.

"You do have a houseful of beautiful cats!" Mr. North said as he looked around the living room.

Princess Margaret gave a loud purr.

"You're welcome," Mr. North said to her.

"I think we ought to drink a toast," Mr. Dawson said. "I have a wonderful sherry I'm sure you'll enjoy. How about it, Mr. North?"

"I'd love it."

Mr. Dawson got the glasses and poured the sherry. "To the lovely Princess Margaret who is going to help America get a good night's sleep."

Elizabeth and Norman toasted with ginger ale. "And to Norman who took her pictures," Elizabeth added.

Norman blushed.

Princess Margaret got a great big bowl of milk, and all the other cats gathered round to share it.